W9-AQT-396

Christmas with Tucker

**Center Point
Large Print**

Also by Greg Kincaid and available from Center Point Large Print:

A Dog Named Christmas

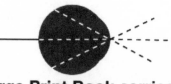

CHRISTMAS
WITH TUCKER

Greg Kincaid

CENTER POINT LARGE PRINT
THORNDIKE, MAINE

This Center Point Large Print edition is
published in the year 2010 by arrangement with
Doubleday Religion,
an imprint of The Crown Publishing Group,
a division of Random House, Inc.

Copyright © 2010 by Greg Kincaid

The text of this Large Print edition is unabridged.
In other aspects, this book may vary
from the original edition.
Printed in the United States of America.
Set in 16-point Times New Roman type.

ISBN: 978-1-60285-926-5

Library of Congress Cataloging-in-Publication Data

Kincaid, Gregory D., 1957–
   Christmas with Tucker / Greg Kincaid. — Center Point large print ed.
      p. cm.
   ISBN 978-1-60285-926-5 (lib. bdg. : alk. paper)
   1. Human-animal relationships—Fiction. 2. Dogs—Fiction.
   3. Christmas stories. 4. Large type books. I. Title.
PS3561.I42526M9 2010
813′.54—dc22
                                                    2010026671

To my grandparents
Chester and Maurine Richardson.
Like all great grandparents,
they finished up where my parents left off.

Prologue

With one paw in the wild and another scratching at the door of humanity, dogs are caught in an awkward spot. It misses the mark to describe a dog as just an animal. We recognize that our pets can be both beasts and evolved life-forms keenly attuned to human needs. Country dogs may be more appreciated for their animal nature—hunting, herding, and guarding—while city dogs are cherished for their humanlike ability to expertly deliver companionship and unbridled affection.

From time to time, for a lucky few of us, we come across a dog that seems to move naturally back and forth from one world to the other. Such a dog can howl at the distant coyote, hunt for his own food, refuse to back down from a charging adversary, and run hours on end with equal glee under snow or sun. In an animal like this, we respect the sheer aliveness that radiates from his eyes. And, when the day's work is done, he'll lay down by our feet, content. For this dog, you know that there is nowhere he would rather be than with you. This dog is complete in both worlds. He models for us how to simultaneously be good and alive—animal and angel.

Frank Thorne owned this kind of dog. He received the four-year-old Irish Setter in exchange for repairs he made to an old tractor. The owner of the broken-down machine had inherited the tractor and the dog from his grandfather. He kept a picture in his wallet of the old man standing beside that proud setter, taken after one of their weekend hunting trips. The snapshot was good enough—he had no room for a dog.

Thorne was too sick, too broken, and too mired in personal problems to know the value of his bargain. The setter spent most of his days tied up outside on a chain attached to a giant steel corkscrew that tightened into a clay loam, binding him to the ground like concrete.

Tethered, he could only watch wild turkeys amble across the meadow, roosting to a setting sun, or rabbits venture from their winter thicket as snow danced across Thorne's barnyard. The dog yearned to experience all that was outside the radius of his twenty-four-foot circle.

From time to time, when Thorne had better days, he would take the dog for rides in the truck, long jaunts along the banks of Kill

Creek, or just let him into his modest, run-down house to enjoy warm evenings by the fire that glowed in an old potbellied stove. Thorne was a lonely man incapable of realizing a friendship with the dog or anything else.

Not long after his arrival, the dog saw a boy walking across the field to the west. He pulled on the chain, whined, and pulled again. His tail wagged, but there was no give. In the late afternoons, before Thorne returned home, he could hear a school bus full of children stop at the top of the hill. The same boy he had seen walking through the fields was on the bus, too.

He saw or heard the boy almost every day until June. As the summer progressed, the boy ventured out less frequently. By August, he did not come out at all. When he heard the boy in the yard, the dog could tell that the boy's energy was different. There was less laughter on the hill.

Things grew worse with the man, too.

Thorne stopped leaving the house and a putrid odor seeped from his pores. The dog knew the smell. He recognized it from his previous owner, who ran a tavern near the city. October turned to November and Thorne became less attentive to the dog's needs. The setter lost weight and the sheen vanished from his red coat. As hunger set in, his disposition naturally deteriorated. He paced nervously.

One day in November, around 3:00 P.M., though it was still some distance away, he could hear Thorne's truck rapidly approaching home. There was another sound farther in the distance that caused pain in the dog's ears. He whined and tried to bury his head between his paws as it grew nearer. It was the sound of sirens.

Impervious to his own discomfort, he wagged his tail excitedly as Thorne's truck screeched on its brakes and turned wildly into the driveway. The truck fishtailed to a stop not ten feet from the dog's run.

The dog did not know what to expect from this tall, gaunt man. In the past, he was affectionate and seemed to value the dog, but lately his master treated him like an inconvenient responsibility. Thorne stumbled out of the truck and, without bothering to shut the door, fell to the ground. This is the position from which humans often play with dogs, so the dog grew excited and ached for a greeting, some acknowledgment of his existence, but there was none. Instead, Thorne pulled himself up, brushed the dirt from his clothes, and made sure the package he so carefully clutched in his hands was still intact.

The pain in the dog's ears grew more severe as the sirens grew closer, but still all he wanted was to be with the man. He ran excitedly at the end of the chain and barked for attention.

It was still early in the afternoon, but not too early for the ubiquitous bottle in the brown paper sack, the bottle that held the scent that the dog now associated with his master. Thorne gripped the sack in his left hand like a lion trainer clutches the whip that separates him from certain death. The red setter whined again and even let out a little yelp, but Thorne still ignored him. Instead, he walked into the house and slammed the front door behind him.

Soon more cars pulled into the driveway; two of them carried the painful siren. The noise ended when the drivers turned off their engines, got out of their cars, and approached the master's house.

The dog was confused. It was rare for other people to enter his area. The strangers' voices seemed nervous and there was a scent in the air that he associated with danger. The dog barked furiously and pulled at the chain.

The uniformed men talked to the dog. They said that they would not hurt him, but still they stayed well away from his run as they approached the house, and he could sense their aggressive postures. He was prepared to lay down his life to defend Thorne from this strange new threat.

The men banged on Thorne's old front door. The dog desperately threw all of his weight at the chain, but still it did not give.

A few moments later, one of the men led his master out of the house in handcuffs, locked behind his back. The dog sniffed the air to assess the potential for danger. There was no odor of blood, but the smell of alcohol, stale and sour, clung to his master. Thorne's head hung down as he walked toward the cars. He said nothing to his dog as he was shoved into the patrol car.

An older man had arrived at the scene and he spoke to the uniformed men in a voice that the dog recognized; he had heard it before from the top of the hill. There was no fear in this one.

The old man went to his truck and pulled out a half-eaten bologna sandwich and tossed it to the dog, eyeing him from a safe distance as the setter devoured the human food. The man approached him, and the dog hunkered down in fear—still uncomfortable with a stranger entering his space. It was not difficult for the dog to trust the old man, who spoke in a deep, soothing tone and brought him food when no one else had. Tired, and exhausted from trying to take care of his master, he rested on the ground. When the man reached out to pet him, he calmed to his touch and rolled onto his back in a submissive gesture.

The old man stood and looked west. The sky was darkening. A difficult winter would soon be upon them.

Chapter 1

Most barns double as family museums. The vertical beams are riddled with the nails and hooks that hold history. Pieces of harness, rusted tools, license plates from old trucks, or a calendar from a bygone era—they all tell a story. It is the task of the curator to pick the right exhibits, to find the single pieces that sum up the entirety of a people, a place, or a time long past.

From the window of our old wooden barn, I could see my son, Todd, throwing the ball to our dog, a mature yellow Lab he'd named Christmas. The engines of both his truck and my wife's car were warming up. Todd's breath was condensing in the cold winter air. We were all preparing for another day's work. For myself, I had an unusual task, one that I had embarked on nearly fifty years ago. It was time to finish it.

I lifted Tucker's leather collar off a hook, the letters of his name faded but still visible. At six o'clock, one of our family's most important museum patrons was scheduled to visit. I wanted to put together that one exhibit that would make the past clear, not just for me but for her, too. To do so, I had to go back to a cold wintery place where I had been reluctant to travel. If I was to assume the curator's role, I had no choice.

Everyone has a winter like that one. A place and time that changes us forever. A place and time when the wind blew so cold that the memories still hurt. It was now time to walk straight through that hurt and excavate an important piece of my life. For her, I would do this work.

The sound of gravel crunched in the driveway as Todd and Mary Ann each pulled out, leaving me alone on our farm. I would have the entire day to focus on my project. It seemed that I had been way too busy the last few decades, often doing unimportant things, to take the time to do something this important. Now the work had to be done.

With the collar in my hand, I walked toward the house.

Once inside, I collected the other pieces that would form the exhibit: an old tin cup from the kitchen windowsill; from the top shelf of a closet, a stack of letters carefully banded together and arranged chronologically, and a tattered puzzle box with hundreds of rattling pieces. I poured myself a cup of coffee, threw a few hickory logs on the fire, and settled into my old rust-colored corduroy recliner, the treasures assembled on my lap. This spot had always been a good place to think, to explore a few crevices and crannies and, if things went well, rejoin parts of myself that had been split apart.

I picked up the tin cup and closed my eyes, waiting until I could feel the steely cold of that winter of 1962 blow across my face and hear the faint rumble of the old truck as it labored up McCray's Hill. . . .

Chapter 2

The truck door creaked open and then slammed shut. The old man walked through the back kitchen door and took off his hat, exposing gray hair cut short. He had high, flat cheeks that were tanned in the summer from hours spent working outside, a Roman nose slightly large but proud, and a complexion that was surprisingly immune from wrinkles for his seventy-two years.

He was an inattentive shaver who apparently believed that using a razor on alternate days was good enough. His eyes were as blue as the Kansas sky and as sharp as a red-tailed hawk.

There was not a suggestion of fat on his frame, which was steeled by work too hard to imagine by today's standards. After fourteen-hour days in the barns and fields, he moved stiffly. The no-nonsense look on his face was as constant as the cuts, bruises, and scrapes on his body.

Now he gently kissed on the cheek the tall, white-haired woman standing at the kitchen sink, and filled an old tin measuring cup with the cool rainwater drawn from their cistern. He tilted his grizzled head back, drained the cup empty, and then let out a long "Ahhh." He repeated this ritual several times a day during their nearly fifty-year marriage. It unfailingly brought a contented smile to her face.

Standing there together by the sink on that early-winter afternoon, they appeared a perfectly matched team, ready to plow through the prairie sod that had sustained generations of McCrays. She was lithe, beautiful, and wore one of her ubiquitous flowered dresses, beneath which radiated a calm goodness that was a wellspring of comfort to all who knew her.

In the summer months, he might fill and empty the tin cup four or five times before his thirst was quenched. Any water that remained at the bottom of the cup he would unceremoniously pitch out the kitchen window onto his wife's jewel-toned flowers, the blossoms of which she chose for one purpose alone: the nectar that best attracted her beloved hummingbirds.

But that day, one cup full of water was enough. Grandpa Bo set the cup down, clutched Grandma Cora's elbow, and pulled her close to him.

In a secretive way, from behind my book, I watched them from my reading spot on the living room sofa. For several months now, I had been hiding behind, or perhaps *in,* my books. That afternoon, I had to leave Tarzan stranded in a tree, so that I could pick up a few words of the conversation between my grandparents, two of the people I loved most in the world and whose house I'd shared every day of my thirteen years.

My grandmother's voice seemed surprised. "Not again. Oh, no. Bo, I'm so disappointed." After letting out a pained sigh, she continued, "I shouldn't be surprised, though, given his state of mind. The poor fellow practically had to raise himself with those parents of his, and he's lost more than he's gained in this life—so many jobs, his marriage, and now a friend."

There was a silence and I could not hear their words until her much louder "You what?"

His baritone voice reassured her. "Don't be upset, Cora. This can work out."

"I'm just shocked, that's all. I never thought . . . Are you sure?"

He grunted. "I stopped being sure of anything on June 15, 1962."

When I heard that date, a sinking feeling came over me. Like December 7, 1941, it was one of a half-dozen dates our family would never forget. After putting my book down, I got up and walked into the kitchen. The talk stopped when I entered the room.

They both looked at me expectantly, so I invented a question. "Grandpa, did you sell the cows?"

"Yes, I sold them, and had lunch at the Ox. Saw Hank Fisher and his wife." He hesitated and then just spat it out. "And I made a stop on the way and brought home a dog."

"A dog!" I had always wanted a puppy and I could barely believe my ears.

"It's not exactly what you think, George, so don't get excited."

"What do you mean?" I asked.

"He's not a puppy and you don't get to keep him. Frank Thorne has himself in a bad spot again. He has to leave his farm for a while. He was your dad's friend and he's our neighbor, so I guess it's up to us to help him out. I'd appreciate your help."

"You mean that mean-looking red dog that he keeps tied up in front of the house? The one that barks like a devil every time my school bus goes by?"

"That's the one."

My idea of a good dog was a friendly puppy. I let my feelings be known in a simple and direct way. "I don't think I want to take care of Thorne's dog."

Bo McCray had the same simple, direct communication style. "You'll do it anyway."

I looked to my grandmother for support, and she stared hard at me in a way that signaled this issue was not up for discussion. "All right, then, where is he?" I asked.

With a tinge of annoyance, Grandpa set his battered tin cup down on the countertop. "In the truck," he answered, pointing toward the back door. "And if he has a name, Thorne didn't mention it."

The old truck was typically parked in the implement barn, but this afternoon it had been left in the gravel driveway close to our farmhouse, so I walked out the back door, without another word. I stopped and stared at the truck for a moment, not sure what to expect and having no idea of the value of the cargo in the hold.

Chapter 3

As I let the kitchen door slam behind me, it occurred to me that, like an elephant or a giraffe, a dog was foreign to the McCray farm. The adult words, spoken frequently by my father and by my grandfather, too, came rushing back to me. *Dairy cattle and dogs don't mix, George. Quit asking for a puppy.*

For years I grumbled about it, as any kid would, but like hot days in February, I accepted that dogs were not part of the McCray landscape.

Now this no-name dog was sitting in the truck and I didn't know what to make of it. Part of me was excited, but there were other, unsettling feelings, too. At that point in my life, I needed the world to be arranged according to rules that I could count on, even when those rules were unpopular.

In my life, the one rule that children counted on most had been broken: *parents don't leave their children.* That rule I considered inviolate. For me, there was an obvious corollary, too: *a boy doesn't lose his dad in a tractor accident on a hot summer afternoon.* My father, John Mangum McCray, was here one morning as he had always been, ate breakfast, went outside to work, and by that afternoon, was gone forever.

Now this *dairy cattle and dogs don't mix* rule was being broken, too. Deep down, I was sure that I would never be allowed to have a dog, and though I resented it, it was still one of the rules that I counted on to keep my crumbling universe in order. It was somehow frightening to see this rule broken. Which rule was going to be broken next? What had I done wrong to be the only kid in my school who had lost a parent? I felt as if I were being punished, but I didn't understand why. Somehow, my father's death spoke some dark truth about me. Surely, good kids didn't lose their dads—only the unworthy and the undeserving are so fated. What had I done?

There was more swirling around in my mind, too. I put my hand on the stock gate release and hesitated before pulling the latch. Surprises had lost their appeal. I just didn't know what to do or how to feel about this most recent unplanned event. The latch release needed oil and it creaked as I opened the rear stock gate. I made a note to myself to squirt some oil on the hinge.

Standing in the truck bed, hesitant but with his tail wagging, was a beauty of a dog. I had never seen Thorne's dog up close. Though he seemed thin and needed cleaning up, he had long red hair and looked to be an Irish Setter. I opened the door fully and reassured him. "It's okay, boy.

I won't hurt you. Come on, jump on down."

He took very little coaxing. He ran at me full speed and jumped. Surprised, I scrambled backward and fell onto my backside. Instinctively, I raised my arms over my head to protect my face from an attack.

This assault was not, however, of a violent nature. In fact, it was more a matter of his smothering me with affectionate kisses and trying to nuzzle me to my feet. The dog put his cool, wet nose to my face as if we were the closest of friends, cruelly separated but now reunited. I laughed and pushed him away gently. "Enough!"

It was no use; he was back on me, demanding attention. I got up and took a few steps, hoping to gain some separation, but he chased after me, nipping playfully at my feet. He seemed to take great pleasure in knocking me to the ground so he could jump back on me and pummel me with canine attention.

Trying a different tactic, I just froze. He backed a few feet away from me and started barking, demanding that I play with him. I started to run away, hoping he would chase after me, but he was so excited that he set out circling the house at full speed, his big, floppy, red ears going up and down as he bounded by me. I wondered if doggie Christmas had arrived early for this pooch.

After two quick loops around the house, he decided to return his focus to running circles around me like an Indian war party, substituting yelps and excited high-pitched barks for war cries. I decided to take the offense and dove on top of him, knocking him down. Before he could recover, I jumped up and ran off. He rolled over, and we began a long game of tag, now both of us circling around the yard at a furious pace.

We wrestled, ran, and played for nearly an hour, until finally the sun began to set. The dog seemed to have endless energy, so eventually I just collapsed on the ground and covered my face with my arms. He rested his head on my chest while I tried to catch my breath.

The back porch door slammed as Grandpa walked out and calmly petted the dog as he rested by my side. He shaped a homemade collar and leash by making a slipknot in an old length of rope and looped it around his neck. "Come on, boy," he said reassuringly.

The dog followed my grandpa obediently. He was a totally different creature now—alert, quiet, and respectful—like he was working and not playing. Grandpa walked him around the yard for a few minutes. Then he led the dog toward me as if to reintroduce us.

They stopped a few feet away from me and, as he was apt to do, Grandpa summed up the dog and my life in a few sentences. "He's a bit older for a *puppy,* but he has great potential. You can practice with this dog for a month or so.

Maybe, after Christmas, when you go to Minnesota, your mom will let you get a dog of your own."

"I'm not sure if I want to go to Minnesota."

"Your mother misses you. She needs you."

My dad wasn't the only rule breaker. My mom had "left" me, too—albeit with my blessing— moving off the farm at summer's end to be near her parents in Minnesota. My sisters were both in college there and Mom, wrapped in grief, simply couldn't bear to be on the farm without my dad. Back in August, when she decided we should move, I asked her if I could stay for a while longer.

I understood that she needed to get a new start on life, but I just wasn't ready to leave. I asked to stay on the farm until Christmas, and she reluctantly agreed. It had seemed so simple, but I was beginning to realize that the plan had grown complicated as each passing day made me question what "home" really meant.

"Don't put me in the middle of this, George."

I took the homemade leash away from him. "The truck gate needs oil. I'll do it."

"Dinner will be ready soon," he said, as if he were relieved to change the subject, too. "It's going to turn cold tonight. After you oil the hinge, you had better plug the heaters into the stock tanks or your chickens won't have water. By the end of the week, it could start snowing, too." He looked down at our new charge. "When you're finished, please put Frank's dog on the back porch, where he can stay warm."

He started to turn away, so I caught his attention. "Grandpa?"

"Yes," he said, turning back to me.

"I don't think Mr. Thorne deserves a dog if he is going to just tie it up all day."

Grandpa paused for a few seconds, considering his words. "I don't know about that. All I know is that Thorne is gone for now. So I did him a favor. Maybe I shouldn't have, but I did what I thought I had to do."

He stood there for a few moments longer, alternating glances between me and the dog. He seemed lost in thought. Finally, he turned away and walked toward the back porch of our old house, but not before issuing one last instruction. "George, if it snows on Friday, as much as they say it might, I'll need you to help with the morning milking while I run the road maintainer. Can you do that?"

Shrugging my shoulders, I said, "Sure, I guess," and walked off to do my work.

Chapter 4

Our family owned and operated McCray's Dairy, which would have passed to my father had he lived, and then on to me. Dairy farming sounds almost picturesque to city dwellers, but in reality it was a combination of some of the hardest things about farming. Keeping cows fed and watered was a giant task—and that was before you even got to the milking part.

In the summer months, the cows foraged in the meadows around our farm for their own food, but to produce maximum quantities of milk, we also provided our small herd with grain year-round. The grain had to be grown, harvested, and stored. During the summer, we also put up large amounts of hay, which is just grass—cut, dried, and put into bales, which can be fed to the cows during the winter months when the fields are fallow.

Watering a herd of cattle is no small task, either. It is essential that dairy cows have lots of water available to them. Each cow drinks between twenty-five and fifty gallons of water a day, depending on the weather. On a hot August day, even a small herd of dairy cattle would need a thousand gallons.

Unfortunately, in the 1960s, rural water service was almost unheard-of in Kansas. Farmers had to find their own sources. We had two: our lake, which was really just a big three-acre pond, and the rainwater that trickled down through the roof gutters and that was stored in large underground concrete cisterns. When the cisterns ran out, which they often did, we had to buy water in town and then haul it to the farm.

Nobody should have to work this hard, but Grandpa, like most small farmers, had a second job to bring in cash. When he wasn't farming, milking cows, or attending to his old pair of Clydesdale horses, Dick and Dock, he was one of three county-road maintainers: he graded gravel and repaired potholes in the summer, and was charged with keeping the snow off the roads in the winter. Grading and farming went together well. There was more farmwork in the summer and less grading to do. In the winter—when there was less farmwork—there was typically more grading. Because it was not as physically demanding, grading was a good job for my grandfather to retire into. At least, that had been the plan until that day in June.

He used a big piece of equipment that most people would describe today as a grader, but back then it was called a "maintainer." He even had an official county designation, "Senior Road Maintainer," but some people called him The

Maintainer, or Big Bo McCray. To me, he was usually just Grandpa.

When I came home from school, I had a specific list of chores that I had to do before dinner. My sisters had their lists, too, but when they left for college, a lot of their work fell to me. First, I had to find and chase stragglers up to the barn. Once all the cattle were near the barn, I shut a big steel gate that separated the barnyard from the meadows and fields that surrounded our farm. I put their grain in feed troughs, and made sure water was available for them while each cow waited her turn to be milked. Electric pumps moved the water out of the cistern and into large aluminum tanks we kept by the barn.

While Grandpa and my dad did the milking, I fed and cared for the remainder of the stock we owned, which included pigs, chickens, and horses. I also was expected to clean out Dick and Dock's stalls. Fortunately, their stalls opened out into an open-air paddock, where they spent most of their time and left most of their messes.

The morning milking was a whole different matter. The steps were the same, but they had to be performed in the dark; the process started at 4:30 A.M. I doubted if I could brush my teeth at that hour, let alone function as part of the milking crew.

I had been exempt from that chore so that I could be attentive at school. No one realistically expected any kid to get up at that hour. Now it looked to me like another rule that I thought I could count on was going straight out the window. It knocked me even more off balance. Most likely my grandfather and I were struggling with the same problem. How in the world were we going to get all of this done without my father's help? For him, the answer was simple. We would work harder. For me, it was not so easy.

On the surface, I felt some resentment at being charged with extra work, but the problem wasn't just the morning milking. As I walked out to the garage to grab the oilcan from the toolbox, the feelings festered.

After oiling the hinge and checking on my chickens, I stood by the back door and stared south out into the meadow, watching the few remaining leaves of autumn fall from an old oak tree and float to the ground like little yellow paratroopers. Fall was over; winter was beginning.

The wind blew harder and I had to button my coat. I stood there trying to figure out what it was beyond the wind that was bothering me.

There was still a melancholy feeling fueled by my grandfather's simple request to help with the work that needed to be done. I sat down on the back porch steps and petted Thorne's dog. Running my fingers through his fur gave me some comfort.

As adults, we forget these confused teenage years. After we've addressed a problem or a feeling a dozen times, resolution becomes second nature. But at barely thirteen, it was all new and still very confusing. Most of us don't get it right the first time. I was no exception. Destiny compelled me to try on the wrong attitude. Knowing how the wrong attitude fits and feels is often the first step in recognizing a better one when it comes along.

At that young age, I could see only so far. Until we mature and develop the ability to get perspective on our problems, we're left in an inevitably selfish and superficial place. That's what makes those teen years so hard.

What was on the surface, staring hard at me that afternoon, was a big question of fairness. First off, I had lost my dad. He was the person I looked to more than any other to show me the path through life. He was the sentinel rock at the top of the hill from which I could take my bearing even in the stormiest of weather. More than anyone else's, when I tripped and started to fall, it was his strong arms that picked me up.

On a deeper level, though I didn't want to admit it, part of me was just plain scared. My grandfather expected me to do adult work—I already worked harder in one day after school than most of my city friends did in a month—and I was still not quite ready to give up being a boy.

I began thinking about how hard my life had been on that farm. And now it was going to get worse.

Maybe it was grieving, maybe it was sulking, or maybe it was just being a teenager and needing to get over my self-pity. Justified or not, I didn't think it was fair that I had to do my own work plus half of my dad's, too. And now, with Thorne in jail, I had to take care of this dog. I wondered if there was a limit to what was expected of me and if I had a say in a darned thing. No one asked me; I was just told what to do.

Sitting there on that back porch, petting Thorne's dog, I felt none of it made sense anymore. My mom was right—this farm life was hard—and things would be much easier for me in Minnesota.

Mom had told me on several occasions that if I changed my mind and did not want to wait out the rest of the fall school term before joining her, she would send me a bus ticket. That was starting to make sense to me. Who could blame me for wanting to spend time with my own mother?

The thought of being with her again caused something in my mind to click into place, like the tumbler on a combination lock, and I was able to go a little bit deeper into the problem. Being so caught up in my feelings of loss for my father, I failed to realize how much I was missing my mom and my sisters, too.

Minnesota was starting to tug on me just as it must have tugged on her.

The dog rested his head on my leg and finally seemed tired. After getting up, I turned my back on a vivid sunset and went inside, disgruntled and confused. Did I love the farm? Was it the last connection to my father and a lifestyle I had valued? Was it my future or just part of my past—another fatality in a barrage of rules that were no longer applicable? Leaving Thorne's dog on the back porch, I opened the kitchen door, went to the sink to wash my hands, and sat down with my grandparents for dinner.

Chapter 5

"George, you've been awfully quiet tonight. Is everything all right?"

"Yes, I think so, Grandma."

I tried to gather enough courage to bring up the subject of the morning milking. "I was wondering how I can do the morning milking and get ready for school at the same time."

Grandpa set down his fork and gave me a sly smile. "Good question."

I pushed the point. "I don't know if I can make it all work."

"Sure you can, George."

"How?"

"Same way I did when I was your age."

"How was that?" I asked again.

"It's easy, George."

"Really?"

"Sure it is, son." He leaned back in his chair and pulled his suspenders out away from his chest, and then rested his giant hand on my shoulder and smiled. "You have to get up early. Getting up early is good for you. I've been doing it for nearly seventy years. These snow days

35

aren't likely to happen more than forty or fifty times this winter."

He gave a little grin and I knew he was teasing me. "Not really, George. It's mostly just big snowstorms that can take a few days at a time to clear. You can do that, can't you?"

Truth was, I wasn't sure I could do it or wanted to do it. I resisted the impulse to say "It'll be hard to help with the morning milking from Minnesota" when the thought of leaving the farm and my grandparents behind became even more upsetting. That would be a very hollow victory for me. I lost my composure and tears formed in the corners of my eyes.

I just stood up and walked out of the kitchen. The sound of a chair being pushed away from the table suggested what I already knew. My grandmother would be following right behind me.

I turned around to face her and she clutched my arm. "George, we'll get up and do the chores together. It'll be all right."

I felt like a little boy and was angry with myself for losing control. At the same time, I needed some comforting and was glad to get it. I wanted to be like my father and grandfather, capable of so much, without a word of complaint along the way. I just did not know how to do it.

"Thanks, Grandma, but I've been thinking. . . ."

She looked at me patiently. "Yes?"

I tried to swallow my words as soon as they came out. "Maybe it's time for me to go to Minnesota."

There was a very brief flash of pain in her eyes and then she smiled in an accepting way. "We're all mad, and sad, and frustrated, and it just comes boiling over sometimes. It happens to all of us." She took my hand and with more love than I could imagine existing in any one person, said, "George, if you want to be with your mother in Minnesota now, we'll make it happen. You go read for a while and relax. Make a decision when you're feeling better. We wouldn't want you to stay here if it isn't where you want to be."

She patted me on the back and I retreated to my living-room fort: a brown sofa with the fireplace on one side and a stack of my library books on the other. I tried to rid my mind of the problem by escaping into a book. Somewhere between the beginning and the end of the story I was trying to lose myself in, another realization surfaced. There were only three members of McCray's Dairy before it lost its strongest partner. My grandfather was struggling hard to take up the slack. If I left, it would be down to a team of one. It would be pretty lonely for him and I didn't want to let him down. I wondered if Grandpa could run the dairy without me and doubted he could afford to hire anyone else.

Chapter 6

Decades later, I would constantly tell my son to remove his ever-present headphones so that I could speak to him. I sounded like a broken record—*"Todd, take those things off so you can hear me."* When I was thirteen, the constant refrain was "George, please put your book down and come in here and talk to us."

At the sound of Grandma Cora's voice, I shook myself into the present and walked into the kitchen. She was finishing cleaning up from dinner and Grandpa was still reading the paper. Without looking up, he asked his question.

"Is this nameless dog of Thorne's any good?"

"Sure."

"What's he like?"

"Well, he seems all tuckered out right now."

With the water running as she washed the dishes, my grandmother misheard my answer, with interesting results.

"Well," she chimed in brightly. "Tucker is a very nice name for a dog."

My grandfather looked up from his paper and smiled at me. Neither of us saw any reason to correct her. So I just went along. "Good a name as any."

"I want to see this Tucker for myself," she said, drying her hands on her apron. She held open the back porch door. "Why don't you come and show him to me?"

I stayed on her heels, curious to know what she'd make of the dog. She knelt beside the setter, who opened his eyes and gave her a trusting look as she gently massaged his ears.

My grandfather got up from the table and joined us. He smiled as she conversed with the dog.

"Tucker, you are a fine dog."

It took less than five minutes. Tucker could say goodbye to the back porch and hello to inside living quarters.

"George, please take Tucker inside right now where we can properly care for him." She followed me into the house and pushed a pile of scraps into a steel bowl. Tucker did not bother to chew much of anything; he just gulped it down. When he finished, he settled down beside Grandma, who'd joined my grandfather at the table, and stretched his paws out in a contented way. She continued to scratch his ears and pet his red coat, praising him for no discernable reason, though she used his new name every chance she could, as if to teach it to him. "Sweet Tucker, nice boy. . . . Tucker, you're going to like it here. . . . Are you still hungry, Tucker?"

Retreating again to the sofa, I left Grandpa in the kitchen reading the paper. Occasionally, he would look over at Grandma with a raised eyebrow as she kept up her patter with Tucker.

It was getting close to bedtime when what remained of my living-room reading time was again interrupted. My grandmother was still in the kitchen, now carrying on an intense conversation with my grandfather that was quickly losing the casual tone that I could naturally tune out while reading. The rising volume of her voice reflected her agitation.

"All of those years of John wanting a dog and you were so stubborn about it—now you bring home a dog. How did you think it was going to make me feel?"

"The dog needed a home. What else was I to do? Besides, I thought it would do George some good."

"George is going to Minnesota and that dog is going back to Frank's when he gets out of jail. How is that going to work?"

"Not so loud, Cora, he'll hear us."

Soon there were muffled sobs from the kitchen.

"Do you want me to find another place for the dog?"

"Bo, it's not that."

"Then what?" he asked.

I heard her let out a long, low moan. "When I

glance at our little George, I see John. It makes me want to bust inside." She tried to hold back her tears, but she just sobbed. "Oh, Bo, even the smallest things trigger memories and make me think of John. First we lost him, and soon enough we're going to lose George, too. He may not even last here till Christmas—he just told me so. Nothing is going to be right on this farm."

"Don't say that, Cora."

"What else am I to think? My insides have been chopped to pieces. I don't understand. How do you stay so calm?"

My grandfather let out his own long sigh and spoke in a determined way. "It's like this, Cora. We can't afford an avalanche. For now, that's all I am trying to do."

"What do you mean, Bo?"

"One loss triggers another, and another, and before you know it, the whole family is busted apart at the bottom of the hill. Just a pile of rubble."

Unable to resist, I peeked, unnoticed, into the kitchen. My grandmother's head was buried in my grandfather's massive chest. She hugged him tighter. "I know," she told him sorrowfully.

"We can't let that happen. I've got to stay tough—for you, for George, and for the whole family."

"You're my granite. You've always been.

Nothing ever has and nothing ever will knock us down from the top of McCray's Hill."

He pulled her closer. "I won't let it." He plucked four or five pins from her hair, loosening it from its knot and letting it fall down her shoulders, the way she wore it at night. He ran his fingers through it in a comforting gesture.

"What am I going to do? I can't go on like this anymore."

"It's November. You'll do what we do every year."

"What's that?" she asked.

"After you make the best Thanksgiving dinner in Cherokee County, you'll waste weeks of time putting up all of your Christmas decorations, just like you always do."

"How can I do that, alone, without John and Sarah helping me? You know how much they loved Christmas. The girls were always the first ones to drag the decorations out of the basement and string the lights. Now they are all gone."

"I'll help you. George is still here. We'll do it, somehow."

"I'm sorry, but right now Christmas seems frivolous."

He held her cheeks in his hands. "You've got more substance than any person I know. There is nothing frivolous about keeping our traditions alive. It may be just what we need to stay propped up. I need you to do it."

I crept upstairs, not wanting to disturb them and feeling vaguely guilty for listening in and watching them. It was only November, but it was cold getting ready for bed. Tucker followed me up the steps and sniffed about my room. I pulled a blanket down from the top closet shelf and put it on the floor. He stared at it and then leapt up onto my bed, apparently not that interested in cold oak floor planks. After shutting off the light and situating Tucker at the foot of the bed, I pulled the covers over my head and tried to get warm. The "Minnesota" debate continued to rage in my head. It was easy to picture my mother near a cozy fire, resettled in the beloved hometown she'd always missed, laughing with family and old friends and enjoying the evening in front of a television, something no one around here seemed to think we needed. I loved my McCray grandparents deeply, but I had fond memories of the Peterson side of my family, too.

My mother's parents lived in a grand house near Minneapolis that was not only equipped with a television but also filled with cousins and an endless parade of friends and neighbors. It was a wonderful place where we had spent several joy-filled summers. Now my mom deserved and needed that love and support. I just didn't know about myself.

When she met my father after the war,

moving to a farm had been a compromise for a city girl who'd fallen in love with a country boy. Though she went willingly, the farm no longer made sense, not for her. The McCray farm was now merely a painful collection of reminders. She agreed I could manage for a few months without her, safe in my grandparents' care, while she resettled our family in Minnesota. After Christmas, which she and my sisters would spend on the farm, I would go back with her to start fresh, too.

For me, though, moving away from the farm seemed like a betrayal of my father. I thought perhaps I'd get over that feeling, but as the weeks and months passed, I could not let it go. There was part of me that hung on to a hope: if I just had enough patience, my dad might still walk right through that back kitchen door. For after all, he had been doing it every day of my entire life. He would be laughing with Grandpa Bo. On his face would hang the outdoors, punctuated with little bits of grease, grass, and dust cemented to his face by sweat and sun. He would be tired, but it was farm-tired: sore muscles, sun-bleached hair, and the ever-present assortment of scrapes and bruises that marked one day of simple toil.

Through it all, over the years, no one ever looked more alive to me than my father when he came home at the end of the day. If it happened, if this was all just really one long, cruel dream, I wanted to be there when the screen door slammed shut and he walked back into our lives.

So I stayed and waited and pretended that maybe tomorrow would be that day. My mother made it clear that she had not wanted to leave me behind, but she understood and allowed that I needed a few more months on that farm. So, in early September and with my full approval, she packed the car and drove off.

With my father gone, my mother moved to start over, my sisters away at college, and my grandparents lost in each other's arms, I was not sure where that left me, but I did know that I felt very much alone on top of that windswept hill.

Before long I could hear, like sand blowing hard against glass, the sound of little bits of snow and sleet tapping out a haunting rhythm on the windowpane. Tucker sneaked up from the foot of the bed and squeezed into the space between me and the wall. He felt warm and comforting.

Tucker's ascent from the back porch and into our home was now complete, but my work was just beginning. Very soon, things would begin to change.

Chapter 7

"Tucker needs his breakfast, too," my grandmother said as she set his bowl on the kitchen floor. He lapped up his food with vigor while we looked on.

"He eats more than George!"

"Very funny, Grandma."

My grandfather stood near the kitchen window, surveying the yard. "All we got was a dusting." He then turned his attention to a quick study of the dog. "He looks better. Food and a comb can do wonders for man and beast alike."

It took only moments for me to recognize what a good dog Thorne had stumbled on to. As I got ready for school that morning, it was clear that both my grandparents had reached the same conclusion.

No one in the house could pass the dog without petting him and making some favorable remark about either his appearance or his friendly demeanor. When I got out of bed that morning, I almost tripped over him. He had spent the rest of the night on the floor, at my bedside. Having a dog felt so normal, if not necessary—it was as if the McCray family had suddenly discovered the benefits of running water.

Looking back on it now, Tucker was the only living creature in our house who wasn't feeling sad, and perhaps that's why he established himself so easily in our hearts and minds. When he wagged his tail and acted content, he reminded us how happiness looked and joy felt. We sensed that there was a huge absence in our lives, and though Tucker couldn't fill it, his presence hinted, gave us some hope, that those vast empty spaces might someday be full again.

On Thursday afternoon, after dropping my lunch pail and books in the house, I trudged around the farm, doing my chores with Tucker by my side. It had been a while since I strayed far from the barnyard, and I thought today would be a good day to do some exploring. Grandpa caught up to us and seemed to have a new project in mind for us.

"Hold him for a second." He slipped a bit of twine around Tucker's neck and roughly measured its diameter, tying a small knot in the twine and stuffing it into his pocket. "I've got some leather scraps around the shop. I'll make him a collar. Do you want to help?"

"Nah, I think I'll take him for a good long walk down to the creek."

Grandpa reached into his jacket and pulled out a letter. "I almost forgot. This is from your mother." He handed the slim envelope to me, along with the rope we were still using for a leash. "You better take this, too. Just in case he tries to run off. Don't let him in the barn when I'm milking. I don't want him spooking the cows."

"I won't. Thanks, Grandpa."

I pocketed the rope and the letter. I wondered if he'd speculated on its contents and how he felt knowing that I'd told Grandma I might want to leave the farm before year's end. I knew that my grandfather, like Grandma, wanted me to feel that I would always have a home with them. I didn't want to hurt him in any way.

As Tucker and I walked away from our homestead, the late-afternoon sun reflected off his brushed coat in hues of deep burnt pumpkin and cinnamon that reminded me of autumn. The clouds hung low in the sky and made the blue space above us seem closer, yet still immense. It was brisk for November, but bearable with a sunny and gentle breeze that carried a musty timber smell up from the creek.

As we walked out of the barnyard, we passed by Dick and Dock. Both of the giant beasts were resting their heads on the top rail of their corral. Tucker ambled over to investigate the pair, but when he got too close, they kicked up their heels and disappeared into the barn.

"Come on, Tucker, let's go."

We headed east along the path that went past

Thorne's cabin. At the edge of the fence line, we turned south, through the hayfields, and down to Kill Creek. Once we crossed under the fence, I slipped the rope around his neck so we could practice working on the leash.

When we got to the creek, I released Tucker and skipped stones. While I counted skips, Tucker sank down to his eyeballs in the creek, holding his head just above the water and lapping up cool drinks of the murky water with his tongue.

While resting in a little patch of grass by the bank, I watched the dog play in the water and tried to take in the pleasing aroma of the wild onions that were the last remaining bits of plant life tenacious enough to stand up to the advancing march of winter.

I pulled the envelope from my pocket, removed the letter, and started to read:

Dear George,

Everyone misses you terribly, but I'm at the top of the list! I like my new job and still can't believe how much they are paying me . . . three times what I made working for the telephone company when I was a teenager. I am enclosing a few pictures of your new house and your bedroom that I thought you might like to look at so they will feel more familiar to you when you get home. The house is only 5 minutes away from Grandad and Grandma Peterson! They spend lots of time over here and can't wait to see you. How are things there on the farm? I'm sure your grandparents are glad to have you around and I know they will miss you very much when you leave. Please assure them that we will all come and visit as much as possible! Trisha and Hannah are still loving college life— especially since they're at Grandad's alma mater and he and your grand- mother join them for all the football team's home games. They were both home for the weekend and insisted that we make "George's Oatmeal Cookies." I told them I would not dare make them until we could share them with you.

Grandma and Grandad Peterson asked me to tell you "hi," too. We'll see you at Christmas. I can't wait . . . miss you so much. I'll try to call you before we leave so we can start planning, packing, etc.

Love,
Mom

p.s. When I come back to Kansas for Christmas, I am going to make you a whole sack of your cookies!

I folded up her letter and put it back in my pocket. The house in the picture seemed huge by our standards and my bedroom was already decorated with a football bedspread and book-shelves. I had always wanted bookshelves in my room.

When I turned to the north, a growing chill was in the air. The sky was going from blue to gray and puffs of darker clouds were rolling in on the horizon. With each gust of wind, the few leaves that remained on the trees were letting go, accepting their place. Unfortunately, I had no such clear convictions. Kansas. Minnesota. Minnesota. Kansas. Where was my resting place?

The dog's nose was deep in a mouse run and his tail wagged rhythmically. I wondered how dogs sensed or thought about *home* and if Tucker might have something to teach me on the subject.

"Tucker, come on. It's time to walk back."

Chapter 8

"Snow day!" my grandfather yelled, his voice booming up the staircase.

Nowadays, when children hear grown-ups say "snow day" they rejoice because it means school is canceled, and they can sleep in and dream of a day spent sledding or building snow forts. But back then, those two words meant something entirely different in our house. It did not necessarily mean that I had no school. What it did mean, I did not especially want to hear at 4:30 on a Friday morning.

Tucker liked bunking with me, and I was happy to have a warm furry thing near me in the early-morning hours. He seemed ready to do his part to make sure I got up on time. Try as I might, he was hard to ignore. Once he heard my grandfather's call, he began yawning, scratching, and stretching.

Already my grandmother was brewing coffee, and when its aroma mixed with that of fried potatoes, eggs, and bacon, it was a strong call to draw me out of bed, though I remained huddled in a cocoon of warm covers for a few more precious minutes.

There was an additional sound on that November morning: the powerful, deep rumble of the diesel engine on the maintainer as it first turned over. As the engine smoothed out, the muffled coughs of that old steel dragon gave way to a roar that was out of place on a cold winter morning.

I could hear my grandfather put the throttle into idle, allowing the engine to warm up; he often let it warm up for a good half hour, especially on very cold mornings. The cab door slammed shut. Grandpa was on his way to the house to make sure I was moving around. There was no need to pull back the curtain from the window; I knew what I'd see outside—snow.

Tucker, now wide awake, sensed that some action was afoot. He pricked his velvety red ears as if to say, "What is this 'snow day' stuff?"

The back kitchen door slammed and Grandpa yelled up the stairs a second time, "Snow day!" I was more than wide awake now, knowing that I'd have to take over my father's responsibilities and do the morning milking, so that Grandpa had adequate time to do his job, too—all before I caught the bus and put in a full day at school.

Tucker jumped off the bed, sensing the work that needed to be done, and looked at me. I thought I heard him say, "Let's go. Don't you know? It's a snow day."

"Not you, too! Okay, okay!" Between my grandfather's calls and Tucker's coaxing, I somehow moved past the adolescent brooding and resentment that had gripped me when Grandpa Bo first laid out the extra morning chores. Egged on by Tucker, I felt the tasks now more of a challenge than an unjust imposition, and I would rise to them—even if I was rising very slowly in this cold weather.

Forcing myself out of bed, I pulled my jeans over the long underwear that kept me warm. All the while, Tucker circled around me impatiently. I scolded him. "Look, Tucker, I don't have fur like you. I have to wear this stuff. You'll just have to wait."

Peering downstairs through the floor grate that allowed the heat from the kitchen to flow up into my bedroom, and which also was our unofficial intercom system, I yelled to my grandfather, "I'll be there in a minute!"

Tucker and I spilled down the stairs and into the toasty kitchen, ready to work. My grandmother hugged me as if she had missed me terribly. Her affection chased away any lingering chill in the early-morning air. She had her winter clothes on and was ready to help out with the milking.

"Snow day," she repeated, holding me tightly. I ate quickly. Grandma Cora's cooking, like glowing embers in the pit of my stomach, sustained and warmed me for hours—if not a lifetime.

There were twenty impatient cows to milk and

only two hours to do it before I had to be ready for school, so Grandma and I got to work in the predawn hours. First, my grandmother filled two buckets with hot water from the kitchen sink and mixed in the special soap we used on the cows' udders and teats to kill any bacteria that could contaminate the milk. I patted Tucker on the head and reminded him that this was the one chore for which he would have to stay behind.

We put on our boots and headed out the back door, each carrying one pail of hot, soapy water that steamed all the way down to the barn in a cold morning air that both assaulted and embraced us.

There were floodlights illuminating the barnyard, so we could see how hard it was snowing. Already, there were two or three inches on the ground.

After pulling off my warm mittens, I lifted the latch from the hook and slid open the south barn door. As I let in the first six cows, Grandma poured their feed into the troughs. There might not have been much variety in their diet, but still each cow eagerly made her way to the breakfast table. To get to the trough, each cow pushed her head straight through the milking stanchions, which I closed behind them so that they were securely in place.

We were lucky, or so my grandfather reminded me. As far as modern inventions went, a close third behind the wheel and indoor plumbing was the Babson Bros. automatic milking machine.

The milk from our cows went first into a large stainless-steel container that was attached to the machine. To the uninitiated, it looked like a giant steel urinal attached to a motor.

As I strapped the Babson Brothers' finest invention to each cow, my grandmother scrubbed away, preparing for milking. My father or grandfather could complete this series of tasks with effortless motions, but with freezing fingers, and less experience, I moved clumsily. It was 6:30 before Grandma and I could close the barn door and call the job finished.

By 7:15, on that Friday morning of our first snow day, I was cleaned up and standing out by the road, waiting for the bus. Far to the west, I could hear the distant roar of the maintainer vanquishing our first snowfall by pushing it to the shoulders that flanked the roads. If it had only snowed a little bit more I might have been able to avoid school. Winter was only just beginning to stretch her legs.

Chapter 9

"Wake up, McCray!"

Mary Ann Stevens pushed me from across the aisle of the bus. She wore her hair in ponytails and though she was a year older was not too snooty about associating with a seventh-grader like me. I liked talking to her on the bus and she seemed to fill in where my sisters left off. She shook me again. "We're almost there."

I opened my eyes in disbelief. "Already?"

The bus had followed the highway and arrived at the Crossing Trails Central School, which housed grades one through twelve. The school was but several years old. Before the county schools consolidated in the late 1950s, I could remember my older sisters riding their ponies to a one-room schoolhouse that was only two miles from McCray's Hill.

The road to the school was clear that morning since the maintainer had blazed through the snow just an hour earlier. I had rested my head against the cold glass window and slept the entire way. My first snow day had worn me out.

As I stumbled out of the bus, Mary Ann continued to tease me. "Sleepyhead, I was talking to you for fifteen minutes before I realized you were asleep."

"Did you say anything interesting—for a change?"

"You'll never know."

I teased her back. "Next time I have a hard time falling asleep, I know who to call."

I had assumed that my teacher, Mrs. Weeks, liked me. That morning I realized I was mistaken. I barely had my coat off when she excitedly made her morning announcements.

"Class, the lead part in our annual holiday all-school play goes to . . ."

She paused dramatically as all the girls commenced oohing and aahing, as if one were about to be crowned Princess of the Kansas Territory.

"George McCray," she said proudly. "You will play the part of our narrator, Santa Claus! Isn't that exciting?"

This was awful. I smiled politely and tried not to groan. Last week she had mentioned the play, and I figured I would get stuck doing something, like building the sets. But this? Memorizing lines would take time and work—on top of all my other newfound responsibilities. Her news was hardly cause for celebration. My male classmates snickered at my "good fortune" until she began casting them as assorted elves, reindeers, and angels, which was even more humiliating.

Mrs. Weeks must have assumed that because

I loved to read, a major part in the school play would fit me nicely and add some much-needed cheer to the first Christmas without my father. If Dad had been around, he would have helped me with my lines, and my mother would have made me a costume and a long white beard. It certainly wouldn't be that way this year.

My teacher was right about one thing—I did love to read, and I was one of the best readers at Crossing Trails Central School, even better than some of the high school kids. Instead of having to read what Mrs. Weeks assigned, I was allowed to choose whatever appealed to me, from Zane Grey to Walter Farley, Dickens to Defoe. Reading was a passion that I'd inherited from my father.

Dad never went to college, but he was far from uneducated and was insistent that we take school seriously. He read paperback novels, from the classics to pulp detective novels, and loads of magazines, his favorites being *Popular Mechanics*, *Sports Illustrated*, *Time*, and *Scientific American*. He remembered what he read, too.

He bought us the *Encyclopaedia Britannica* from a silver-haired traveling salesman who drove a long black Buick, wore a striped suit with a red bow tie, and swore up and down that with these encyclopedias the McCray children were virtually assured of success in their chosen endeavors.

For three years, my father stayed up long nights

reading all the volumes. His mind traveled over a wide range of subjects the following morning. At breakfast, the conversation was as likely to cover wheat prices and weather as the feeding habits of orangutans or the farming techniques on an Israeli kibbutz in the Negev desert. My sisters typically acted bored, but Mom would always say, "Hush, girls, it won't hurt you to learn something."

My father read stories to my sisters and me every night, even when the girls claimed to be too old. Mom would walk in and out of the room and simply smile. I think she enjoyed watching him read to us as much as we enjoyed being read to. He chose rollicking adventure tales, animal stories, classics, and even fairy tales that always seemed to be just right for all three of us. Those evening reading sessions were among the things I missed most about Dad.

Although it was hardly compensation for being cast in the play, Mrs. Weeks did give us a free period later that day, encouraging us to start learning our lines. But I decided to write to my mother. We had a lot of catching up to do.

Mom,

It's been a busy week. I have really been missing you. I'm just not so happy here on the farm, without you and Dad. I had to get up at 4:30 this morning to do the milking and Grandpa has LOTS of snow to clear. It's not that bad getting up so early, but I really don't like it that much. I'm taking care of Frank Thorne's dog. We named him Tucker—Mr. Thorne never named him anything, as far as we know —and I like him a lot. I got the part of Santa Claus in the school play. I hate that, but Eddie Sampson has it worse. He has to be an elf and wear red tights. Happy Thanksgiving—ours will be a quiet one, but we can't wait to have you here for Christmas.

Love you and miss you so much,
George

Though I used the letter to let off steam about the extra work, my goal was simply to let Mom know how much I loved and missed her. I purposely stopped short of telling her that I couldn't wait to move to Minnesota, and that I was considering taking her up on that offer of a bus ticket. Writing it down on paper felt like a real commitment, and a reality I wasn't ready to confront. Once again, I wondered fleetingly what would happen to the McCray Dairy if I left it behind. How would it be for Grandpa Bo and Grandma Cora to be alone on the farm?

On the bus ride home that afternoon, I tried to memorize my lines, but it was hard to concentrate. It occurred to me that if I left Kansas before Christmas, I would get out of having to play Santa. Somehow, though, the idea of leaving just to avoid memorizing a bunch of words didn't do much for me. The wind shook the bus and we had to drive slowly to avoid the snow that drifted across the county roads. I knew that my grandfather would be out late into the night. I did not know that very soon he would have a reluctant helper.

Chapter 10

"Grandma, I can do the milking on my own today."

Complaining to my mother seemed to have purged some of my resentment. Besides, it was Saturday morning, so there was plenty of time.

"Thanks, George. I could use the rest." She sat down in her chair. Scratching Tucker behind the ears, she pulled him close to her. "Tucker and I will have a cup of coffee and wait for the sunrise."

When the work was done, I rested inside, but I quickly grew bored, so I bundled up to walk Tucker—the part of my dog-sitting responsibilities that I enjoyed the most. Tucker loved to walk, too—so much so that in the days to come, it would seem almost cruel to deny him his outdoors time. That Saturday we ventured to a place where we would return many times.

My family always called it Mack's Ground, though Mack was an early settler who had long since died. Decades earlier the land had passed into the hands of Mack's descendants, who lived in Texas and didn't pay much attention to their Kansas holdings. Tucker and I made it our private park.

Mack's Ground was a thousand acres of timber, creeks, and secluded meadows that started out just east of Thorne's house and went on for several miles. They were mysterious and ancient acres. While Mack's collapsed old cabin was worth digging around in, my favorite place was Mack's Lake. It was bordered by forest and filled with bass below the water and ducks above. The lake was built by the WPA in the 1930s. The banks were lined with stones, which made it perfect for fishing.

My grandfather told me that lots of lakes were built in that period just to keep men busy. As a young man, in his spare time, he himself ran a crew of horses that worked on several local lakes, including Mack's Lake.

Tucker was eager to point a rabbit or a covey of quail, though I wasn't much of a hunter. Lighting out after a squirrel or a woodchuck was more fun for Tucker than any game of fetch I might devise.

The best part of our journey was always returning to the lake, and that was where we invariably ended our late-afternoon scouting missions. Tucker loved to play along the shore. It was not yet cold enough for ice to cover the lake, so I skipped stones across the surface of the clear water and watched clouds pass overhead like herds of galloping white stallions.

Thinking about the week's events as my rocks careened across the glassy lake, I made a mental note to tell my dad about the school play. And then I remembered. When I remembered, I just sat and felt very empty. The world seemed like such a big place, and I a very little occupant.

Chapter 11

Thanksgiving came and went, and it was, indeed, a quiet one with just the three of us, Tucker, and too much food (most covered with Grandma's gravy). The snow had come and gone, but mid-December was now upon us, and the reprieve was not to last.

One afternoon as the snow was falling again, and Tucker and I ambled back to the house from Mack's Ground, I heard the phone ring. A few moments later my grandmother appeared on the back porch. "George, it's your mother on the phone. Long distance!"

After knocking the snow off my boots, I raced inside to take the call from Minnesota. Today, a long-distance phone call is commonplace, but in 1962 it was an event.

It seemed like a scene from my old life—Mom talking to me after I came in from an outdoor romp. The only difference was that now her voice seemed riddled with sadness.

"I got your letter. I sure miss seeing you, too, George."

"Thanks, Mom."

Sounding as if she'd been crying right before

she'd called, she continued, "I haven't been feeling like such a good mother lately, running up here to Minnesota and letting you stay behind. I don't know what I was thinking."

"It's okay. I asked you to let me. Remember?"

"I thought that being with Grandma and Grandpa was what was best for you, but maybe not. I didn't want to pull you away from your grandparents and the farm before you were ready, but maybe you should come up here now and not wait for the fall term to end. What do you think?"

Her suggestion was in line with what I'd been thinking, but I hesitated. I wasn't ready to pick up and leave right now, and in that moment I resolved to stay as originally planned.

"Mom, it's only another few weeks until Christmas," I began.

"Can you wait that long, George?"

"Yes, I'm okay," I assured her, but clearly she was not.

"All right, then. I suppose I can wait, too. We'll have a fun Christmas together, then head home. Now, tell me about Frank Thorne's dog."

I was thrilled to change the subject and talk about Tucker.

"He's about the best dog in the world. Tucker goes everywhere with me, except school, and Grandma says he whines for an hour after I leave."

"He sounds wonderful. I can't wait to see him. Tell me something else . . . What do you want for Christmas?"

For the first time in my life, I had not thought about it. I knew what I wanted, but no one could deliver that. "I don't care. Anything is fine."

"George, you're quiet today. Are you sure you're all right?" she asked.

"Sure, Mom, I guess so."

"Are you looking forward to the move?"

"Sure, Mom, I guess so."

"Is that all you know how to say?"

I laughed. "Sure, Mom, I guess so."

"All right, then, tell your grandparents hello and we'll see you soon. I love you, George."

"I love you too, Mom."

Not an hour later, the phone rang again. Grandpa was still out working, so the sheriff just left a message. Thorne was getting out of jail and his court date was a week off. My grandmother marked the hearing date and time on the calendar they kept by the phone.

I tried not to notice.

Chapter 12

It was 9:00 P.M. before my grandfather parked the maintainer in the barnyard after going over the roads one last time and came inside for a belated dinner. With Grandma Cora's help, I'd finished the evening milking. Tucker detested being left behind, tied up on the back porch or left in the kitchen, but he had no choice in the matter. Dogs and dairy cattle don't mix.

"Still snowing," Grandpa substituted for a greeting, stating the obvious. Tucker met him at the kitchen entrance, tail wagging as if he was happy my grandfather had made it home safely. Grandpa bent down and drove his cold hands deep into Tucker's fur and pulled him close, allowing Tucker to nuzzle into the gray stubble that grew on his neck.

"How much snow?" I asked.

My grandfather stood up and looked across the room at me. His eyes seemed tired. "Eight inches total for the last two days, drifting deeper. How did the milking go?"

My grandmother answered for me. "Don't worry, Bo, George has it under control."

Because my grandfather was not a talker,

starting a conversation with him was no easy feat. Saying something like, "How 'bout them Yankees?" would get you little, if any, response. With my father gone, he talked even less. The good thing was that when Grandpa Bo did talk, he usually had something to say, and everyone in the room would drop what they were doing and listen carefully.

Now he said nothing for a long time. Finally, he just nodded his head up and down real slowly and said, "Good."

"Will we have school tomorrow?" I wondered aloud.

The first person my grandfather called after dinner was Mr. Bangs, the principal at Crossing Trails. Mr. Bangs always followed my grandfather's advice on whether or not the roads were safe for the school buses. Forget the person who could push some secret red button in the White House. As far as I was concerned, the most powerful individual in the world was my grandfather; he was the one man who could pick up the phone and say, "No school."

Even if I did have to do the morning milking by myself on a snow day, school closings and downed phone lines meant adventure and excitement for me. It was a fair trade. I would take Tucker to explore Mack's Ground in the snow. It would be easier to read tracks and it would be far more fun than memorizing lines for a school play.

"Grandpa," I began, thinking that a little guidance from me could be helpful, "think about how bad it would be if a school bus got stuck in the snow. All of those poor little first-graders— they couldn't walk through eighteen inches of snow without freezing to death."

He just grunted. "Appreciate your concern, George, but I said eight and not eighteen."

After reading and setting tomorrow's clothes next to the heating grate to warm, I climbed into bed and tried to fall asleep. Tucker would join me when he was ready. Through the floor grate, I could hear my grandparents talking in the kitchen. If I concentrated, I could follow the gist of their conversation.

"If it keeps up like this, there will be no ambulance or fire service for much of the county."

My grandmother's voice was full of concern. "People might need medicine. There could be families without food or electricity for weeks on end. We could lose heat. And without heat, water lines will freeze."

"More is coming, Cora. It could be the worst snow in fifty years."

I was listening, as children at that age are still apt to do, hoping to catch a word or two about something else that was on my mind.

For as long as my memory served, the biggest day of my life was Christmas. Although my mother had brought it up briefly on the phone, no one in this household had mentioned it to me and it was only two weeks away. I did not know how to feel about Christmas this year.

What I wanted was going to be hard to bring down the chimney. It was an important conclusion I reached that night when thinking about a Christmas wish list. How do you ask for your old life back? Why couldn't things be like they were when my father was with us and we all lived under the same roof?

Christmas, it seemed to me, wouldn't be any good this year. How could it be when you were thirteen years old and knew, just knew, you were not going to get what you wanted?

This thinking about what I wanted and how I was not going to get it brought about an unpleasant realization. We all come to it eventually, and we forget about how much it hurts the first time it sinks in. As painful as it is, it's probably the first and most important step in growing up.

I remember very clearly that it came to me that night. Not getting what you want for Christmas is really an introduction to one of those facts of life that adults must face.

There was this vague but growing conclusion settling in my young mind that life does not always bestow upon us everything we want or think we should have. We are forced to move away from hoping others will give us what we want, to a new place where we must discover how to find happiness on our own. Santa was the last vestige of youth where all of our wants are magically delivered by some *other*.

Once again, a rule I considered inviolate had been disregarded. Christmas would be anything but the best day of the year for me.

It was like being in the middle of a really great Zane Grey novel, and when I got to page 100, just as I victoriously led my mare over the top of a windswept hill after outwitting the bad guys, someone switched in fifty pages of the bleakest scenes by Charles Dickens and messed up my perfectly good life.

Why couldn't things just be the way they used to be? I'd reached that awkward moment when a child—on the brink of young adulthood—realizes that he is not the center of the universe and is entitled to very little in this life unless he goes out and gets it for himself. From my still childlike perspective, Christmas was doomed to failure because no one could give me what I wanted.

Tucker finally decided to come upstairs. He whined and wagged his tail, and I coaxed him up onto the bed. He was fully capable of jumping up on his own, but he usually held out until I gave him permission. "Come on, Tucker, you can do it."

His warm body helped make me feel safe and

secure. I pulled him close to me, buried my face in his coat, and realized that all I could do was hunker down and get through the winter. I would just have to accept that things did not always turn out the way they should. Maybe that was the new rule.

We rested quietly, and right before I fell asleep, things got worse.

"Cora." I heard the words come up through the grate.

"Yes?"

"George has done a great job with Tucker."

"I know."

"I'm proud of him."

"So am I."

It was quiet and then my grandfather's words came up like thick, dark smoke. "Tomorrow is Thorne's hearing. Assuming he's coming home, I suppose he'll want the dog back."

Grandma let out an exasperated sigh. "I suppose so."

Yeah, that was the new rule. Things don't always turn out the way they should. It made no sense to me that Frank Thorne—a man I still viewed as a loser—should have a great dog like Tucker, languishing on a chain, when I could give him a good home, where he would be loved and well cared for.

A good home—I just didn't know where it would be.

Chapter 13

The next morning I heard the maintainer fire up, but no one was rushing me out of bed, yelling "Snow day! Snow day!"

This meant that my grandfather had decided that the roads were bad enough to necessitate school closing. I guess my concerned pitch for the first-graders of Cherokee County had found a receptive audience. Grandpa had no idea how long it would take to open up all of the side roads and county lanes. He just hoped that the snow would stop soon.

Although McCray's Dairy had been spared, power and phone lines were down elsewhere. Until the roads were cleared, service trucks could not make repairs.

There were only a few road maintainers in those days. My grandfather was responsible for clearing the entire southwestern section of the county, and he had to make the most of the hours he could work the maintainer before even worse weather or total fatigue set in. Now more than ever, he had to "get at it."

I was fine with trading the drudgery of a school day for a few extra hours of laborious milking.

Besides, my grandmother allowed me to start an hour later. Lying in bed till the genteel hour of 5:30 made the milking chores seem tolerable. Throughout the task, I couldn't help but wonder how Thorne's hearing would go, or if it would be delayed because of the snow.

After the milking was finished, I came inside and tried practicing the lines from my play, with Tucker at my feet, and read my favorite books by the fire. The day passed quietly, though Grandma Cora and I listened anxiously for my grandfather's return as the light began to fade. He'd been home for lunch, but we hadn't seen him in several hours.

Finally, he returned, with Tucker greeting him once more as if to say, "Where were you? We were worried!" Still, neither of my grandparents had said anything all day about Thorne's hearing. At dinner, Grandpa announced that there would be several more snow days and at least another day, maybe two, of additional school closings. Ordinarily I would have rejoiced, but I was increasingly worried about Tucker's fate.

"Before you go to bed, George, I want to talk to you." It was coming. My grandfather was not the type to orchestrate a conversation, so I assumed it could not be good. I tried to stall as I washed up and brushed my teeth, knowing that the subject matter of our talk was predictable. I went downstairs near the warmth of the fire and waited for Grandpa to look up from his news-paper. He seemed to be stalling, too, and his eyes were pained.

"George, you've done a good job with Tucker."

"Thanks, Grandpa."

"I spoke with Thorne today. They had the hearing, even with this rotten weather, and he's out of jail and back home. He asked me to thank you and says he'll come around and fetch Tucker tomorrow."

A fury gathered up inside me that I had not expected. "That's not fair. Why should he get him back? He doesn't even know how to take care of that dog."

"We both know you're going to Minnesota. It's been good for you having Tucker around, but it's time to move on. You knew at the start he wasn't yours to keep, remember?"

"I could take him with me."

"It's pretty simple, George. Tucker is Thorne's dog."

With angry tears on my face, I stood up and walked out of the room. Once again, nothing seemed fair. Bit by bit, everything I loved was being taken away from me—Dad, my old life on the farm, Tucker. Bitterness and resentment rose up from some dark space in my mind and I did not know where to put it.

Chapter 14

The following morning, after the milking was completed and with school still closed, I decided to spend the entire day with Tucker, back on Mack's Ground. The idea of running away with Tucker, before Thorne could fetch him, had come to me the minute I woke up and now, as I was closing the barn doors, it gripped me.

In my often still-childish mind, I envisioned fixing up Mack's old log cabin, hunting and fishing for food, and fashioning clothes from animal hides. However unrealistic my dream was, I spent the morning cleaning up the cabin and making a mental list of what I would need for repairs to my new home. By late morning, the wind started to blow the snow and the absurdity of what I was planning finally sank in. For starters, there was one glaring omission from my plan of frontier survival: heat.

By noon, I had given up on running away. I sat down to lunch with Grandma Cora and she asked me what I had been doing. Although I may not have had the courage to run away, I did muster the strength to talk about it.

"I was wondering if I really have to go to Minnesota. Maybe I could move into Mack's old cabin with Tucker and the two of us could live back there."

"How would that work?" she asked with no judgment in her voice.

"With Tucker, I could hunt and fish for my own food."

My grandmother wisely ignored the limitations of my plan and tried to get at what she perceived to be bothering me. "Are you tired of living here with us?"

"No. It's not that."

"You're at the age when young men start dreaming about being on their own. Do you think that's it?"

"Maybe."

"George, your grandfather and I love having you live here and we are going to miss you very much when you leave for Minnesota."

It surprised me the way it just came tumbling out like someone knocked over a glass of water. "I don't want to move to Minnesota, but I don't know where I want to go instead."

She was quiet for a long time and I knew she was carefully choosing her words. "Sometimes, all of us wake up and wish we were somewhere else. That's natural, too." She laughed and said, "When it's cold like this, I usually think about Florida."

She took my hand. "George, you know something we all learn sooner or later?"

"What?"

She then told me something that I always remembered years later with a chuckle.

"George, honey, you don't have to run very far to run away."

She smiled and pulled her hand back. "You know someday this farm was going to be your dad's place, and now, with him gone, it'll be yours. Of course, it's up to you to decide if you want it. No one is going to make you take it. And if you're worried about what'll happen to the McCray Dairy when you're in Minnesota, now don't you be. We'll manage."

I didn't say a thing, so she continued. "You love the dog, don't you?" She found the missing voice for my thoughts that I could not locate on my own.

"Yes."

"You're mad about having to give him back and things just don't seem very fair right now, do they?"

"No."

"I remember when your grandfather first brought him home and asked you to be responsible for him. You resented it, didn't you? It's funny how things change. A few weeks ago you thought it was unfair that you had to take care of Tucker, and now you think it's unfair that you can't do it."

"That was before . . ."

"Maybe you should talk to Frank Thorne. Maybe the two of you could work something out. Who knows, maybe he would let you keep Tucker until you left. It's only a few weeks. He might not mind if you took him for walks after school. I bet there are options here you haven't even thought about."

"You want me to talk to Frank Thorne?"

"Sure, why not?"

"I don't like Frank Thorne." That was my way of *not* saying that I was uneasy around the man. More than once, I'd heard my dad say, "Frank likes his privacy." And, there were all of those stories about the Thorne family—how his grandfather had been little more than a horse thief, his dad a shiftless gambler.

"Why, I've known Frank Thorne since he was a baby. Did you know that Frank and your dad used to be friends in high school?"

"I guess."

"Just because he has a drinking problem, that doesn't make him a bad man."

Before I could think much more about it, the subject of Christmas came up. She stood, walked over to the kitchen window, put her plate in the sink, and turned back to me.

"George, what would you like for Christmas this year?"

I squirmed a little and realized that I did not

81

want to answer her question. "I don't know, Grandma. What do you want?"

"I've never known you to be without a Christmas wish list. Surely there's something you want."

"I haven't been thinking much about it."

"George, you and I are having the same problem. It's been awfully hard getting into the Christmas spirit this year. What are we going to do about it?"

She was right about that and we both knew it. "I don't think I want to have Christmas this year. Christmas is for little kids."

She put her hands on her hips and scolded me ever so slightly. "I am not a little kid and I still like Christmas."

"I don't know, Grandma."

"I know what will help us. Let's you and me cut down a tree this afternoon."

"Sure," I said halfheartedly, thinking how ruined this holiday already seemed. Why didn't Grandma just give up on Christmas? Before I could ask her, we were interrupted by the ringing of the telephone.

Grandma answered it. "Hello, Frank. . . . Sure, that'll work just fine. I think George would like to talk to you about the dog, too."

She hung up the phone. "Frank will come by tonight to pick up Tucker." I felt like someone had reached down my throat, grabbed my heart, and gave it a big yank. I went into the living room and just sat.

Knowing that it was coming did not make it any easier.

Chapter 15

Grandma did not tolerate my moping for long. She insisted that I bundle up and go with her to find a Christmas tree. In years past, this would have been fun. Today, it was a chore. Tucker tagged along for a while, but soon took out after a rabbit and decided to go on his own hunting expedition. He may have been a half mile off on Mack's Ground, but I was sure he could smell or hear us tromping along and would come bounding back when he was ready.

We pushed through the snow until we reached the woods that flank Kill Creek and where wild cedar trees grow like weeds after a summer rain.

Though it was snowing, it was not particularly cold. I carried a handsaw and we trudged along, with Grandma rejecting most of the specimens as too big, too small, or poorly shaped. She was ambling and enjoying the walk.

"George, you know this is going to be a hard Christmas for all of us."

"I know." Of course I knew.

She kept making excuses to hug me. "I sure do like school closings. I am going to miss you when you have to go back."

"I'm going to miss you, too."

"Let me tell you one thing that makes Christmas fun for me."

She had a big smile on her face and looked different all bundled up and walking outdoors. I could see a side of her that was playful and young and sad all at the same time.

"What's that, Grandma?" I stood with my hands on my hips and tried to catch my breath. Trudging through the snow was hard work. It amazed me that she kept up with so little effort.

"Thinking about that one special thing that someone might enjoy receiving that they did not even know they wanted. Like this Christmas tree, George; it might be just what you need— that one thing that gets you in the spirit."

She stopped and stared for a long awkward moment. Although I was not sure, I thought maybe she was trying not to cry. As she spoke, her words cracked in a few places. "I bet a perfect tree is just on the other side of the creek waiting on you."

"Do you think the ice is frozen enough for me to walk over?"

"I'm sure it'll be just fine. The water is shallow there. Go across and pick out the one you want. I'm getting a bit cold and may head back."

We had really not talked about how or why, but it seemed that Grandma Cora had led me right up to the west creek crossing. This was a place I had been avoiding.

As I walked over the ice and through the clearing in the woods that led to the meadow on the other side, I realized I was now standing in the place where Dad's accident occurred. I had been pushing the details out of my mind for months. Now, standing there in the meadow, I felt reality flowing over me and that day in June came blowing back in my face.

My mother was cleaning the kitchen and my grandmother was quietly working at her puzzle table. I was sorting through baseball cards on the living-room floor. My sisters were in town, working at their summer jobs.

Grandma Cora complained to me, "This one is the worst. The pieces are so small and the shapes irregular. I think your mom and your sisters have given up on it."

My mother yelled to us from the kitchen. "George, Cora, come in here. They're at it again!"

We had seen the hummingbird acrobatics many times before, but we wouldn't deny the combatants an audience.

Grandma and I joined my mother by the sink. Two male hummingbirds were fiercely attacking a third in an effort to drive him away from the flowers. They hovered, darted, dashed, and generally moved—horizontally and vertically—through the air with astonishing speed. Theirs was a well-thought-out battle plan. And as with all good plans, position on the battlefield was everything.

As we watched them zooming in and out of view, we saw my grandfather running up to the house, his face white. Instantly, we all knew that something was terribly wrong. When he threw open the back kitchen door, he hung his head as if he were pained to the bone, breathing hard. My grandmother took one look at him and ran to his arms. "What is it, Bo?"

He shook his head back and forth, as if to say no. "I'm so sorry, it's John, he's, he's . . ."

"What is it? What happened?" my mother pleaded, rapidly losing control.

My grandfather faced them both, his legendary strength drained away. "There's been an accident. The tractor flipped. John was killed—"

My grandmother screamed, and my mom buried her face in her hands, crying over and over again, "Oh, my God, no, not John!"

It was the worst day of my life in that house. It was as if the walls of our home, our lives, our very souls, just collapsed.

My father was cutting a field of alfalfa when it happened. The purple flowers attract bumble-bees. He had been mowing near the bank of the creek when the tractor kicked up an entire nest. There were bites all over his body. He must have been fighting them off when he lost control of the tractor, which went over the creek embankment. He was thrown from the cab and hit his head on some rocks. He tumbled into the creek, and the tractor rolled over him, pinning him under the water.

My grandfather, wondering why the tractor had been quiet for so long, set out to check on his son. Good partners have a way of watching out for each other. It must have been terrible for him to have a vague worry change instantly into an unspeakable truth.

Six months after that day in June, I found myself standing in the same place my grandfather had found my father's body. It was a place I pretended did not exist—the place where all the rules were broken.

That running-away feeling came over me again. Suddenly hating everything about the farm that stole John McCray from me, I never wanted to see another field of hay, milk another cow, or touch another tractor. If I could, I would just get on the first bus for Minnesota and never look back. No one would blame me. The absolute finality of death was sinking into my young mind.

As much as it hurt, I accepted that my father was never going to walk through the back kitchen door again, no matter how long I hung around the McCray farm. There was no reason for me to stay here for another minute, thinking that he would.

Using the saw, I cut down the first tree I focused on, angrily hacking away at the trunk. When I finished, I grabbed the tree by the trunk and started to walk back toward the creek.

As quickly as the bitter resentment had welled up, it vanished. It was as if someone just pulled a plug and it all drained out onto the ground. In its place, there was nothing but loneliness.

Dropping the tree and plopping down in the snow, I had a long-overdue conversation with my dad. It was time to sort things out and tell him how I felt.

I love you, Dad, so much, and I miss you every minute of the day. I have this dog, Tucker, and he's been helping me out a lot. Well, he's not really mine but I sure wish he were. You'd like him, I bet. And I'm so grateful to have Grandma and Grandpa helping me out, too. But no matter how hard I try to stop feeling sad and lonely, I just can't help it. I try to stay busy—I'm doing the milking by myself on snow days, and I'm even in this stupid school play. But I don't know how to go about it all without you here. And I don't know if I should stay here or go to Minnesota. I miss you giving me advice. I miss you reading to me. And I'm really sorry for not doing all those chores when you asked.

"What are things like where you are, Dad?" I said out loud, with tears on my face. "Do you think I'll ever see you again? I sure hope so."

How I wanted his strong but gentle hand on my shoulder to tell me it would be all right and that all of these unbearable feelings would pass, and the world would operate by the rules again.

Listening hard, I was hoping for some sign. And then I remembered something he said to me many times before he died. He said that I should take the best parts from the men I admired the most in the world, add them all together, and then try to be that person. One thing I admired about both my dad and my grandfather was that when things went poorly, they always got back at it and tried again. They were both men who valued perseverance.

I realized that if he could talk to me today, that is what he would tell me. I could hear his voice in my ears just as if he were standing there on the bank of the creek. And if I tried hard, I could feel his touch on my shoulder, too.

No matter how bad the roads, George, we just climb back up on the maintainer and try to clear the way. That's all we can do.

So, right there, I gathered my resolve, stood up, wiped the tears from my face, and made a resolution not to give up.

As I brushed the snow from my jeans, something moved at the top of the hill where we collect wild Easter lilies in the spring. I thought it was a deer, until I heard a bark and saw a dog running full speed after a rabbit. It was that big red Irish setter coming to join me.

Before long, Tucker's efforts were rewarded. A rabbit dangled from his jaws. He looked very proud and perhaps he sensed my sorrow, for he suddenly dropped his prize at my feet.

Some people might think it was an unimportant gift, but I knew that for Tucker, there was no greater offering. I had gotten my first and perhaps only Christmas present that year. He was trying to give me the most valuable thing that existed in his world. He was trying to make sure I stayed alive when doing so might mean he would go hungry.

I leaned over to scratch him behind his soft, floppy ears. "Thank you, Tucker. Thank you for being my friend."

It was time to go home, so I dragged the tree back across the creek. It was probably too big of a tree, particularly to haul a half mile back up to the house. But if Grandma was right and a tree was going to fix my Christmas, it was going to have to be a big one.

After I crossed the creek, I looked for my grandmother, thinking she might still be out walking, but she was gone. I could see her tracks leading back to the house. Seeing her solitary footprints, I sensed her own brand of sadness and was reminded of something my mother told me before she left. She said I mustn't ever forget that however hard it was for me to lose a father, and for her to lose a husband, it was just as hard for Grandma Cora and Grandpa Bo to lose their only child.

That night Grandma Cora put little bits of Tucker's rabbit in with the pot roast, and we offered him a plate of his own as our thanks for his sharing, and as a treat for his last dinner with us. After a brief discussion, with all of us trying hard to keep our emotions in check—even Grandpa—we'd decided that it was only right that Tucker should go back to his owner. After dinner, I think each of us said our private good-byes to Tucker. All I could do was sit with him on the living-room floor, stroking his red coat and feeling the warmth of his body. I had no words for how I felt.

It was very cold and dark by the time Frank Thorne pulled into the driveway.

Chapter 16

Frank Thorne was in his mid-forties, thin, and had a blond handlebar mustache that went well with his cowboy boots and hat. He smiled shyly as he stood at the back door, gingerly stepping into our warm house. Tucker looked at Thorne and wagged his tail, but he stayed at my side.

When my grandfather extended his arm to shake hands, Thorne had to pull his hands from his pockets. His fingers were stained with black grease. "Welcome home, Frank."

"It feels good to be back."

"Do you have any work laid out yet?"

"No. Not yet." He remembered that his hat was on and he hurriedly removed it. "Hopefully, I'll have something soon."

"Well, I might need some help on the maintainer, if this weather keeps up. You interested?"

Thorne paused. "I think I should have something come through any day now, but thanks for asking." He looked at me and continued, "George, I understand you've taken care of my dog for me."

"Yes, sir. I have."

"Well, thanks." He looked at Tucker, who was

still waiting patiently at my side. "Come here, boy." Tucker wagged his tail and approached Thorne, but not before I gave him one final pat on his silky head. Thorne knelt down and petted the dog. "Good to see you, Red."

I could feel Tucker slipping away from me and I'm sure I sounded pretty desperate. "Mr. Thorne, I was wondering if you might sell me your dog?"

He looked at me dumbfounded. "Sorry, son, but I'm not looking to get rid of him." He slipped a chain around Tucker's neck. "Looks like you two have become pretty good friends, so you can come up and play with him anytime you want."

For the first time in my life, I wanted to rip the limbs straight off another human being. My face turned red as a pie apple. Grandma put her hand on my shoulder. "Well, thank you, Frank. I'm sure George would enjoy that. You take good care of yourself."

It was just more than I could stand, watching Thorne head out the back door with Tucker. My grandparents and I were silent as we listened to Thorne's truck pull out of our driveway. Suddenly, afraid I was going to say or do something I would regret later, I stormed out the back door. Once again, I had an overwhelming urge to run away from all this, but I had no destination. I simply stood in the dark, snowy yard, burning with anger despite the cold. I did my best to collect myself, for the sake of my grandparents, and after a while I went back inside. I still felt powerless and confused.

The next morning, when the bus drove by Thorne's house, I sunk down into my heavy winter jacket so Mary Ann wouldn't see the upset in my eyes. Tucker was tied up, resting beside Thorne's old brown truck, on a snowless patch of ground. I wanted to jump off the bus and take him, bring him *home,* but I knew that was impossible.

No matter how bad the roads, George, we just climb back up on the maintainer and try to clear the way. That's all we can do. I was trying to climb back up, but I just kept slipping. The path ahead was growing harder to follow.

Chapter 17

That afternoon, I got off the bus at Thorne's house to visit Tucker. The brown truck was gone, but Tucker was in his usual spot outside, tied to the post. After knocking on the door and getting no answer, I sat on the ground by Tucker. Wanting him to know that I had not abandoned him, I held him in my arms for a few moments, wondering how to best negotiate with Thorne. Finding Tucker a good home was proving just as hard as finding the right one for me.

Thorne's house was a mess—the paint peeled down to exposed wood, tires and car parts in the yard, and lumber strewn all about. The place looked scary to me and unsuitable for Tucker.

Armed with paper and a pencil from my book bag, I wrote a note to Thorne, opening with a little bit of salesmanship.

Mr. Thorne,

I know Tucker is a handful to care for, so if this dog is too much work for you, I'm still interested in buying him. I'm leaving for

*Minnesota in a few weeks, so let me know
soon if you're interested.*

Your neighbor,
George McCray

I stopped short of telling him that Tucker
deserved a better life.

After searching for a place to leave the note, I
decided to tuck it between the old, ripped screen
door and the wooden front door, with its dirty
glass window. As I opened the screen door, I
could not help trying to look inside. As I pushed
my nose against the windowpane, the front door
swung open—it was unlocked. Thorne correctly
surmised that there wasn't much worth stealing.
Standing on the threshold, letting my eyes adjust
to the dim light, I looked around.

It was as I suspected: chaos. The house appeared
to be one big room with a bathroom and a bedroom at the back. There was a table covered with
beer cans, newspapers, and bottles. On one wall,
there were some photographs I could barely
make out. One looked somehow familiar, but it
seemed so out of place that it made no sense.

Before walking in to investigate further, I
called out, "Mr. Thorne?" No answer. Wanting a
better look at that photo, I took a chance and
stepped inside. Trying to avoid piles of dirty

clothes, broken car parts, and half-eaten bags of potato chips, I walked closer to the wall of photos.

I peered closely at the photo. It was a picture of my dad as a young man with his arm looped around Frank Thorne's shoulder. It looked like they were working on some old car, covered in grease, with broad smiles across their faces. Not understanding why my dad would want to be friends with Frank Thorne, I hurried out the door and pulled it shut, with my note stuck in the doorjamb.

Although it nearly killed me to do it, I turned my back on poor Tucker and walked home. I couldn't bear to say goodbye. He barked frantically and I felt awful for betraying that poor dog. I had no idea what to do or how to make things right.

During dinner, it was easy to avoid discussing what had happened with Tucker that day, as none of us seemed to want to raise the subject of the latest missing member of our household.

Chapter 18

The next morning I woke to the sound of the back door quietly shutting. I reached out for Tucker, but of course, he was not there. I heard my grandfather's work boots as he stepped slowly across the kitchen floor and pulled a chair away from the kitchen table. There was no "snow day" announcement, as there had been for much of the last week.

Why was my grandfather sitting alone in the kitchen with the lights off at this hour?

Huddling under the covers, knowing that something was wrong, I noticed an eerie yellow glow coming up through the floor grate. I could hear Grandma in the kitchen now, but still, they were uncharacteristically quiet. Worried and curious, I got out of bed, but when I tried to turn on the lights—nothing. We'd lost power.

After quickly dressing in the dark, I went down the stairs as best I could with no light. My grandparents were at the kitchen table, talking quietly. An old kerosene lamp with a gaudy Victorian shade rested in the center of the table.

"Good morning, George." My grandfather pushed a chair toward me. "Sit down and let me tell you what winter has blown our way." He chose his words appropriately as gusts of wind shook our house. There was a serious tone in his voice. Grandma Cora squeezed my shoulder as she rose from the table and started to make breakfast.

"George," my grandfather continued, "we have our work cut out for us today."

"Yes, sir."

"Another sixteen inches of snow fell last night and, as you've already figured out for yourself, we lost power. We still have the phone line, but that might not last much longer. We'll have to be extra careful about keeping the ice cracked on the pond and we'll have to milk by hand—just like when I was a boy. It's going to get a little uncomfortable around here. Can you help us out?"

This had to be serious or my grandfather wouldn't have taken so many words to say it. I had seen sorrow cross his face, but until that morning, I had never seen fear in his eyes or heard worry in his voice. My grandfather was comfortable barking orders, but this was different. Until that morning, I had never heard Big Bo McCray ask any man for help, and certainly not a boy like me.

There was only one answer to the question. "Of course I'll help. What can I do?"

"If you'll go down and crack the ice on the

pond, I'll start the milking. Later today, I'll show you how to drive the maintainer. The only way to get through this is to take turns, working in shifts, night and day, until we dig out of this storm."

"Drive the maintainer!" I said, nearly falling out of my chair. This was a big step up from milking alone. I felt a mix of fear and excitement.

"He's only thirteen!" my grandmother warned. "Bo, I told you earlier, it's not a fair thing to ask him to do." Her voice cracked and tears began to fall.

"He's old enough, Cora, and you know I need his help."

"Then I'll take a shift driving, too," she said, wiping her eyes. Like many farmwives, Grandma could drive a truck on a dirt road and a tractor across a field, but I couldn't recall her driving the maintainer in a snowstorm.

"Cora, you're strong, but you can't handle this. And you need to stay and take the emergency calls and help George with the milking when I'm gone. You'll have your work cut out for you, too. I'll take two shifts to his one. That way I can sleep a few hours. Let's eat now and we can start to work at first light. George, you'll start by cracking that pond ice."

Certainly there was better help around somewhere in Cherokee County, but I was available, and Grandpa McCray thought I was the man for the job. Maybe my grandfather was just used to partnering with McCray men and wanted to keep it that way. It felt good to be trusted, though I still could hardly believe he was about to trust me with the job of driving the maintainer.

"Use the twelve-pound sledge and make sure the hole is plenty big. You'd better bring a shovel so you can dig down to the ice."

These were my grandfather's last orders as I set out for the pond from the back door of our old Kansas farmhouse. It looked as if the entire sky had lost power, too; only a weak diffused light passed through the blowing snow and steel gray clouds. I wore rubber boots that were a good protector from the snow and the pond water but were poor insulators, and my toes were quickly cold. The weather turned harsh and unforgiving as it swept down from the north. No jacket could keep you warm, and the cold was only tolerable if you kept moving.

Intermittently, when the sun poked through, there were strong, defined shadows on a winter white pallet of freshly fallen powder. I suppose it might have been a nice day, if you were a caribou or a polar bear.

As I walked down to the pond, the daunting task of driving the maintainer weighed heavily on me.

Chapter 19

The drifting snow was up to my hips as I pushed my way to the pond, dragging the shovel and the sledgehammer. As I walked, I followed a path to the water that the cows had already trampled down. Every time I veered off the path, I stumbled into a little ditch or ravine hidden by the sea of snow.

In the winter months, because they were not foraging for grass, the cattle spent most of their time in the barnyard. We kept water for them in heated stock tanks. But with the electricity out, the tanks would freeze and they would have no other choice but to wander down to the pond for water.

In the brains department, cattle are way below horses and pigs. If they can't find a water hole, they'll wander onto the ice looking for one, and sometimes they'll break through and make their own opening to drink from—a farmer can only hope it happens near the bank, where it's shallow. Every few years some poor cow won't be so lucky. If it's cold long enough, she might wander out toward the middle of the pond toward deeper water. When the ice breaks, she can't get out. This is another reason we kept the stock tanks by the barn and why my grandfather wanted me to make sure there was a large, clear opening.

At the water's edge, I found a small hole the cattle had been using. I used the shovel first to clear the snow away from a four-foot-by-four-foot opening near shore. The ice was smooth and clear beneath the snow.

I raised the sledge and brought it down hard on the surface of the ice. The sledge seemed to only glance off the frozen surface, with sparks of ice blasting into my face. I looked down at the half-dollar-size dent and tried again, and still again, with little result to show for my efforts.

It seemed that the ice was more determined and a lot tougher than I had given it credit for. I tried again, this time closer to the small opening the cows had made on their own, and had some success. I was able to break off a piece the size of two bricks. I pulled the piece of ice out of the water and in the process soaked my gloves.

From that small beginning, I grew encouraged and chipped away, but still, it was not nearly a large enough opening.

With visions of Paul Bunyan and Babe the Blue Ox in my head, I swung down as hard as I could. The sledge glanced off the ice and twisted out of my control. The next solid object it came into contact with was my foot. Even though the ice absorbed much of the force, it still hurt, sending a jolt of pain up my leg and knocking me clean off my feet. After letting out a yelp, I fell, bottom down, into the very hole I had cut into the ice. This was not going well.

I was hoping that no one could see me in this most ridiculous of positions, seemingly resting my backside in a giant frozen toilet bowl, when I heard the first howls of laughter.

"Are you okay?" my grandfather asked between spasms. He had been standing there all along watching me, holding a sixteen-pound sledge in his hand.

"I guess. I sort of hit my foot."

"What did you do that for? You were supposed to break the ice and not your foot. And, George, if you needed to use the pot, you should have gone back up to the house."

My grandfather let out another laugh from the deepest part of his belly and offered me his hand. I stood up, sore foot and all, looked at my wet backside, and laughed right along with him.

It was nice to see my grandfather laugh. I hadn't seen him do that in months. I teased him right back. "Well, what are you standing around for? We've both got work to do."

I swung the sledge again, this time with force and control, as much as anything to prove that he had not chosen a boy for a man's job.

He bellowed, "Good shot! We'll do this together, like old-time railroad workers."

He brought his sledge down hard on the ice. It was as if our pond had become a bass kettle-drum, booming in the early-morning hours.

Soon we found a rhythm and chunks of ice gave way to our assault. My grandfather used the shovel to flick the blocks of ice out onto the pond's surface. When we had the four-foot area cleared, he knelt down in the snow to catch his breath.

His voice took a serious tone. "Do you remember when Mr. Riley lost eighteen head, all drowned?"

"Yes, I remember."

"It's an important job I'm giving you. Do you understand?"

"Sure."

"Until we get power, can you keep this hole wide open?"

I nodded my head up and down. "Yes, I can do it."

"Now that we have the hole cut, it'll be much easier just keeping it clear of ice. Why don't you go inside and change your clothes. When you're ready, we'll start the hand-milking."

As I put on dry things, I thought of the maintainer again. I knew more about hand-milking—which wasn't much—than I did about driving that big machine. But I would let Grandpa teach me in the order he saw fit. I joined him at the barn and we let the cows in, six at a time.

Once in the barn, each cow buried her wet, steaming snout into the trough filled with the feed that we stored in the grain bin for the winter. While they enjoyed their breakfast, my grandfather and I went to work on the other end, milking the old-fashioned way.

Bo McCray could milk twice as fast as any man alive and certainly faster than me. By 7:30, we had all of the milk up and into the cooler, where it would stay until we could move it to the end of the driveway. Though the cooler could not refrigerate the milk since we had no power, it was still cold enough to hold it at the right temperature.

I asked my grandfather, "Why aren't we putting it out by the road for the dairy truck?"

"Until you and I get the roads cleared, there won't be a dairy truck or a school bus or much of anything else getting through. You can go inside and stay warm. I'll start the maintainer and meet you in the driveway."

This was it. He was expecting me to actually drive the maintainer in the snow. Farm boys operate machinery, big machinery, by the time they are thirteen, and I was no exception. I'd learned to drive a tractor as soon as I was tall enough to reach the pedals. But this was more involved. This machine was enormous and even in 1962 probably cost my grandfather as much as a small house. The county paid him by the hour to operate the machine, but he owned it.

A machine this big surely needed a pilot of similar proportions. Besides, I would be expected to navigate it on roads and not through empty, flat farm fields. It was an entirely different set of operating rules. I did not even have a driver's license.

I had ridden with both my father and my grandfather in the cab of the maintainer many times before. On a couple of occasions, during the summer months when they were just grading gravel, they had let me operate the grader on my own, but they were in the cab with me, so there was little risk. It seemed like it was "just for fun." This was for real.

I was very confident that I could grade gravel on a warm day, but grading snow, alone, was a different matter. There was something else, too. As I was walking up to the house, Grandma Cora's words came to me. "It's not a fair thing to ask him to do."

My father had been killed working on a medium-size piece of farm machinery, and now my grandpa was asking me to climb on the maintainer—the biggest, most dangerous, and most difficult machine parked in the implement shed. At first I'd been flattered that Grandpa was trusting me to do this, but now I was downright scared, not sure this was a fair thing to ask of me. Maybe the time would come when I could do this, but now?

As I changed my clothes, these doubts continued to race through my mind. As cold as it was, a clammy sweat formed on my back. When I got ready to leave, my grandmother handed me a sack with cookies and two thermoses—coffee for my grandfather, hot chocolate for me. She tied a scarf around my neck. It was one that my sister had given to my dad last Christmas. She gave me a long hug. "George, *please* be careful."

"Grandma?"

"Yes?"

"I want to help, but I'm not sure I'm ready to do this. Not yet."

She grabbed my shoulders and looked me straight in the eyes and smiled. "If you don't want to do it, just don't do it. He'll ask someone else. He might not like it, but he'll understand. There will be more snow to plow in Kansas on another day."

I don't know why, maybe because I trusted her so much, but I wanted to be totally honest with her. My voice had one of those embarrassing cracks as I told her exactly how I felt. "I'm kind of scared."

She put her arm around me again and pulled me tight against her. "Of course you are. You should be."

"I don't want to disappoint Grandpa."

She looked at me very seriously. "The choices we make when we are young can define us for the rest of our lives. There is nothing wrong with being cautious."

I choked out my words. "How do we know?"

"If your mind can't tell you, then either trust your gut or follow your heart."

I had been struggling trying to figure out a lot of things in the last few weeks. For once, something difficult made sense to me. Instead of trying to figure out where to live my life, I needed to concentrate on how to live it. My grandfather's request for help was like an ancient horn sounding from a mountain-top—a call to courage. It reverberated not in my ears but in my soul.

In the future, I would have to answer the call alone. This time, the first time—the most frightening of times—I had my grandfather to stand beside me when I answered the call.

I kissed my grandmother on the cheek, pulled on my hat and gloves, and smiled the biggest, most confident smile I could muster.

"I've got work to do." I turned and walked out the door and in some ways never came back.

That morning in December, I became a maintainer. Lifting the blade, adjusting the angle, correct grading speed were all subjects introduced by Big Bo McCray before we left the driveway. But it would be many years before I realized what was really being taught. My grandfather was giving me a new book of adult rules so I could shred the childish primer that had so let me down that year. I learned to become suspicious of rules rooted in entitlement and my needs, and to instead respect rules mortared by truth and concern for others.

The memories of the days that followed, of working side by side with my grandfather, would carry me through other times in my life when I needed to heed the call not just to maintain roads but to maintain my life—times when I needed rules that would never let me down.

Chapter 20

My grandfather took one task at a time and tried to explain as we moved down the road toward town. "The transmission exchanges speed and power. The lower gears give you more power to move heavier loads of snow, but with less speed. You'll do most of the grading in third gear, unless the snow is deep; then, you should use second."

There was a lever on the right of the driver's seat that adjusted the blade height. "I want you to listen very carefully as I lower the blade just an inch."

I felt the maintainer's engine struggle and our speed reduce slightly. The sound of snow coming off the road was interrupted by occasional pings of gravel bouncing off the blade.

"Now look behind you at the stream of snow coming off the blade. What else do you see?"

"Pieces of gravel mixed in with the snow," I said as I glanced over my shoulder.

"That's right. In the summer months, Cherokee County spends a lot of money putting gravel down on these roads. They don't want the McCrays spending the winter months putting it in the ditch."

"Now listen again. I'm going to raise the blade a few inches above the perfect height." The maintainer seemed to surge forward and the engine was less burdened. "Now turn around and look again. What do you see?"

"The maintainer's tires are leaving a trail through the snow."

"Good boy, George; that's when you know the blade is too high. You shouldn't be leaving enough snow for the tires to form big tracks."

"Makes sense."

"George, there is something else you need to know. This is a big, strong piece of machinery. If you take it where it's not supposed to go, you will get into trouble."

I was painfully aware that he was alluding to my dad, but I asked anyway. "What do you mean, Grandpa?"

"You've got to know exactly where you are on the road at all times. Too far to the right or the left and you can drop a tire into the ditch and get stuck, or worse. If you don't watch ahead of you, you can hit a car. If you don't watch behind you, you can't tell if you're doing your work right."

"How can I watch all four directions at once?"

"You can do it. It just takes practice. Go slowly at first, until it comes naturally to you." He slowed down, turned left down a county lane, and brought the maintainer to a stop by the side of the road. He opened the maintainer door, moved off the seat, and stood tall on the running board. "Well, scoot over and give it a try."

I stood up from the small space to his left where I had been perched and settled into the driver's seat. My grandfather nodded at me to proceed, staying on the running board. Stretching my legs out so I could reach the clutch pedal, I placed the transmission in third, opened the throttle, and slowly let out the clutch until it reached the friction point. With the door open, snow and cold air was blowing into the cab, but I ignored it and tried to chart a course down the lane. I looked at the road in the rearview mirror and could see my tracks, so I inched the blade down a little.

Before I had gone too far, my grandfather gave me some more instructions. "Practice starting and stopping a few more times and try to keep the left edge of the blade in the dead center of the road. That way you'll clean the entire road when you come back at her from the other direction."

When I looked behind me, I could see that I was not staying on a straight course but was meandering on and off the center line. "I'm having a hard time keeping it straight."

"You're doing fine. Just draw an imaginary line on the side of the road and keep your right wheel right on top of it."

By midday, after a few dozen instructions and corrections, my grandfather and I had cleared Moonlight Road, Prairie Center Road, and Four Corners Road. We were now ready to head home for lunch.

That morning it seemed my grandfather spoke more words to me than he had in the months leading up to December, and he seemed very pleased with my grading.

Over lunch, my grandmother went over the list of emergencies phoned in by locals.

"The Rathers' daughter is pregnant and the due date is only a week off. They are worried about getting to the hospital and hope you can keep their road cleared."

"Sherry Rather," my grandfather mused. "That would be off of Waverly Road."

"Do you know Waverly Road?" he asked me. "It's south of the highway and north of Lone Elm Road."

"Sure, I know that stretch and I know right where the Rathers live."

My grandmother picked up the next note. "Mrs. Slater only has two days of insulin left. She lives just off the highway on Crossing Trails Road."

"Yeah, I know where that is, too."

My grandmother turned to the last scrap of paper. "Old Mrs. Reed called and wants to make sure you don't forget her."

My grandfather rolled his eyes. "I just cleared her driveway two days ago."

My grandmother laughed and said, "You know how those old people are, worrying all the time."

"Cora, Mrs. Reed is only four years older than me!"

My grandmother smiled but said nothing. My grandfather took out a piece of paper and drew me a map. "George, take a look at this. Does it make sense?"

I looked it over and I knew exactly what he had in mind. "Sure, Grandpa. I get it."

"Now, take your time and do a good job. I am going to sleep a few hours and when you get back, you rest up and I'll do another shift. Do you have any questions?"

"Just one."

"Yes?"

"What if I have a problem? A breakdown?"

"You're never going to be more than about eight miles from home, since we're in charge of an eight-mile radius of roads. So, if need be, you can walk home. There are extra gloves and hats in the cab. Stop at any neighbor's house, if you need to, and they can try to get you home. I've been clearing snow for twenty-five years with that old beast and she hasn't let me down yet. I wouldn't worry."

He then turned to the sink and filled his tin cup with water and handed it to me. "Drink up."

My grandmother gave me a sack of her choco-late chip cookies, refilled my thermos, and sent me out the back door to clear the roads of Cherokee County.

Forgetting all my fears and feeling as if I'd grown five inches that morning, I pulled open the door to the cab, put the maintainer in gear, eased out the clutch, and started down the driveway on my first solo job. Going a little slower than necessary, I built my confidence one step at a time, heading east.

As I passed Thorne's shack, I slowed down to get a better look. His brown truck was there, but Tucker was no place to be seen. Thankfully, Thorne had enough sense to keep Tucker inside in this snow. I wondered if he was ignoring my note or even if he'd been sober long enough to think about it.

The maintainer thrust the snow away effort-lessly. Still, I had a hard time keeping the blade centered in the middle of the road, and more than a few passersby must have wondered if old Bo McCray was losing his touch.

There were few drivers out that day, but those I did see waved and seemed surprised to see me behind the wheel. The sight of Bo McCray's grandson on that giant maintainer was probably enough to discourage them from any further use of the roads.

While I graded, my grandfather did the afternoon milking. Around five o'clock that evening, approaching home, I slowed again near Thorne's place and looked for Tucker. Thorne's truck was in the driveway and Tucker was tied up outside, but this time closer to the porch, where he at least had some shelter from the snow. He must have known it was me, for he pulled on the chain, wagged his tail, and barked in a familiar way. I considered pulling in but thought it might only make things worse, so I headed up the hill and called it a day. Before going inside, I checked with Grandpa to make sure he didn't need anything. He sent me, sledge in hand, down to crack the ice on the pond.

Once a quick dinner was behind us, Grandpa headed back out to refuel the maintainer from the three-hundred-gallon diesel fuel tank we kept by the barn. With a full tank, he climbed back in the cab, pushed the throttle wide open, and didn't quit grading until early the next morning.

Lying in bed that night while he worked, I remember being a little skeptical about Grandpa's nighttime grading. I had tried to plow in the dark before. Even with headlights, it was very hard maintaining a straight line and an accurate plow depth. Grading in the dark would be even more difficult. Still, I had a lot of confidence in my grandfather and told myself that he was up to the task.

We repeated this same process the next day. It

was still snowing, but not as hard, and Grandpa looked tired. While we did the milking together, he told me about the old days when he had to maintain the roads with horses, like Dick and Dock. He said it was slow going, but there were fewer roads.

The horses could not move snow this deep and the county would be left waiting for a thaw. It was different then; people were more self-reliant, and there was no electricity and no phone lines or ambulances in the county. It didn't matter much if the roads were clogged.

He kept the harness and the old horse-drawn blade stored in the implement shed along with other McCray prized possessions: an International Harvester and a Massey Ferguson tractor, plows, cultivators, seed drills, rotary and sickle-bar mowers, hay rakes and balers.

Some of the farm equipment was new, most was old, but all of it was constantly breaking.

The old road blade had not been pulled by horses for decades, but from time to time my grandfather would ride Dick or Dock, most always in the Crossing Trails Pioneers' Parade each spring.

My guess was that he kept the horses and old blades around for a reason. If the maintainer ever broke, he was prepared to clear the roads with horses, though by 1962 they were far too old to do the job. If the horses couldn't pull the blades, he owned countless shovels and we would get at it one scoop at a time. Some people might have described him as stubborn, but that was only part of the story—Big Bo McCray was a fighter.

Chapter 21

The next morning, after I finished milking the cows and clearing the ice on the pond, my grandfather and I went to the barn. He asked me to remove a milk can from the cooler and help him pour it into twenty sterile glass bottles. What was left in the can he took outside the west barn door and let spill out onto the ground. "What are you doing?" I asked.

"The dairy trucks can't get through and the cooler is full. The dairy won't accept milk that's not fresh."

"Aren't we keeping the roads clear enough?"

"We're doing fine, but the other county maintainers are behind. They have not been able to get north to the dairy road and the last six inches of snow has really slowed them down. The dairy can't take the risk of coming this far out and getting stuck. If that happens, they lose an entire day of collection. It's safer for them to wait until the roads are better."

"Why don't we help? We could do the road to the dairy for them. I can do it today. Right?"

"Getting through to the dairy might be what's best for us, but there are others in this county that we have to think of, too. How would it look if I did what was good for us and ignored all the other people that have needs?"

"Not that good."

"That's right. We have a list of priority roads that have to be cleared first and the road to the dairy does not happen to be one of them."

After we sat down to a quick breakfast, he drew up another map and put two large milk crates on the table. Not only did I have roads to grade, but I also had deliveries to make.

"People can't drive on the roads and we've got milk to give away. I will put twenty quarts of milk in the back of the maintainer in the crates. There's already a box in there with eggs and other staples. I'm collecting extra food and supplies along the way from our neighbors and trying to redistribute to the families that don't have enough. With more and more phone lines down, and roads blocked, people are short on basics."

"What do you want me to do, Grandpa?"

"I want you to pull into every house you pass and clear their driveway for them. Most of the farmers have small driveway blades they pull behind their tractors, but with the maintainer you can do in two minutes what would take them all day. Next, get off and knock on the door; try to make sure everyone is getting along all right. Offer them anything they need from our supplies and try to collect back their extras in exchange, including empty milk bottles, so we can refill them." He hesitated and looked up at me. "Can you do this, George?"

I hesitated for just a moment. Tired and unaccustomed to working so hard for so long, I needed a break. My grandmother's words were still lodged in my mind. This was getting to be very hard work and still I couldn't help wondering if there wasn't someone else who could do it better than me. It seemed to me that my grandpa and I had to do all of the work for the entire county. While I wished my dad were here to help, I knew what he would tell me. It was our job to take care of the roads. It was our duty to help our neighbors. *Just climb back up on the maintainer, George, and clear the way.*

"I'll do my best."

"We need to move faster, George, before things get worse. I have a few tricks saved up for big storms. First, let's bring up the blade and leave three inches of snow on the road. Cars can push through a few inches and we can move faster the less snow we have to push. You should be able to stay in third gear that way. Next, we're going to clear one lane on all the major roads. We'll come back and clear the other lane later."

"That way the emergency trucks can at least get through?" I asked.

"That's right. But here's what you need to do. We're creating a lot of one-lane roads. The

123

problem is when two cars meet, no one is going to want to yield the right-of-way for fear of getting stuck. There will be problems."

"So, what do we do?"

"First, I want you to ask everyone to stay off the roads for forty-eight hours and give us a chance to get both lanes cleared; essential and emergency driving only. Next, every quarter mile or so, you'll need to back up and create a wide space, like a turnaround, where two cars can squeeze by each other."

"I can do that."

"You can follow a half mile or so of what I did last night and get a better idea of what I mean. George, there are two priorities today—things you have to do."

"What?"

"First, you've got to get the road cleared into town so the fuel truck can get out here and deliver us more diesel. We've got only a two-day supply left."

"Okay. What else?"

"There's insulin in the box for Mrs. Slater that I picked up from Dr. Richardson last night. She has to get it today. She could get real sick without it, maybe even die. Do you remember where she lives?"

"Crossing Trails Road."

"That's right."

My grandmother handed me a bag lunch and a

thermos. She kissed me and said, "Be careful, George."

"Don't worry, I'll be fine." I said these words as much to convince myself as to convince her.

On that cold December morning, I set out clearing the roads my grandfather had outlined on the map, stopping at each house along the way. My first stop would be the hardest of all. Frank Thorne's house.

Chapter 22

With the maintainer in second gear, I pulled into the driveway. From the placement of the tire tracks in the snow, it looked like his truck was stuck. As my grandfather had requested, I graded his driveway, such as it was, parked the maintainer, and mustered my strength to knock again on that old front door to make sure Thorne was not in dire need of supplies.

Tucker immediately started barking, but I could tell it was not an anxious or cautionary bark. He knew it was me and was just excited. I knocked again, but still there was no answer.

I opened the door slightly and was greeted by Tucker trying to push through to the porch. Though I wasn't an experienced dog owner, I recognized the whines of a canine that needed to get outside and do its business. After a moment he came running back to me and I opened the door again, letting him back into the house. He was jumping up and down excitedly. It seemed that he was missing me as much as I was missing him. I leaned in across the threshold. "Mr. Thorne, are you home?"

The house was dark and the morning light

was not strong enough for me to see well. I pushed Tucker aside and stepped in and gave my eyes another second to adjust to the dimness. I tried again. "Mr. Thorne, are you here?"

I heard a wheezing noise. By the door, there was a small table with a lamp on it. I found the knob and tried to switch it on. Thorne had lost power, too. The only light came from the dying fire in a potbellied stove.

Even in the shadows, I could tell the room was dirtier than it had been the last time I was there. Frank Thorne had not let Tucker out and the dog had left a mess or two of his own, which added to the stench. No wonder he'd been so desperate to get outside. On the sofa in the corner, not far from a window, Thorne looked up with a half-dazed stare. "What do you want, boy?"

I felt myself quiver.

"Go ahead, boy, spit it out." He seemed impatient.

"Mr. Thorne, my grandfather asked me to stop by. I mean, I'm grading the roads. We're taking shifts because of all the snow. I graded your driveway for you. He wanted me to stop in and make sure you were all right and see if you needed anything. I've got some extra milk and eggs, if you need any."

He struggled into a sitting position. "I am too sick to eat a thing. Come over here, kid."

As I approached, I realized how icy cold the

room was, its only heat source the dwindling embers in the stove. No wonder he was sick. I tried to navigate around the mess on the floor. When I got closer, I could see that Thorne was trembling.

"I got that note of yours. So you want my dog?" His tone was scornful.

Of course I wanted Tucker, but I didn't like the way he asked the question. "I think I could take real good care of him."

"That dog is the only thing I got that is worth a plugged nickel to me." He looked around and waved his arms. "This ain't no palace." He called to Tucker. "Come here, Red."

To my surprise, Tucker wagged his tail and went to Thorne's side. The sick man ran his hands through his coat and talked to him affectionately. "You're a good boy, aren't you?"

He looked up at me. "I tell you what, George; you drive that maintainer up to Wild Tom Turner's place, on Blackberry Hill, and you tell him that old Frank Thorne is in a tight spot and needs two bottles of his best . . ." He hesitated and added, "Medicine. You bring that back to me and then we'll talk about my dog."

He pulled his blanket around him and said, "How 'bout that, kid?" He coughed and collapsed back into the sofa. He was definitely sick with something, but I wasn't sure if this was the alcohol or something else.

"I'll think about it," I said quietly. I'd never heard of Wild Tom Turner or Blackberry Hill and I wondered if it was worth it.

"Don't think too long, boy. While you are thinking about it, throw a couple of logs into that stove."

I spotted some kindling and opened the stove door and tossed it in. It was not enough to make much difference. "Do you want me to bring in more wood?"

"Ain't more, unless you're going to chop it. You just bring me my medicine and old Frank Thorne can take care of himself."

Having work to do and feeling uncomfortable, I turned to walk out. "Goodbye, Mr. Thorne." However hard it was to leave Tucker behind, I was glad to be out of there. Bending down before opening the door, I pulled Tucker close to me and whispered, "One way or another, I'll get you out of here."

When I stood up and turned back around to face Thorne, I couldn't help but sneak a glance at the picture of my dad and Thorne. It still made no sense: the man I respected the most and the man I respected the least in the same picture.

I climbed back onto the maintainer and headed east. Having so much work to do helped to reduce the number of times a day I thought of running away with that dog.

All of our neighbors were grateful to see me,

and they wanted me to come in and get warm, but I told them that I did not have time. They all wanted to know what they could do to help. I explained about the food and the staying off the roads, and they handed over any extra food or supplies they could spare—matches, bacon, flour, lanterns, and more.

I pulled into the Fisher driveway next. Hank Fisher knew everyone in the county. It occurred to me that he could confirm the suspicions I'd been trying to push to the back of my mind. "Mr. Fisher, do you know a man named Tom Turner who lives someplace called Blackberry Hill?"

He was quiet and looked at me in a perplexed way. "Now, tell me this, George, why do you need to know that?"

"Frank Thorne asked me to pick up some medicine from Mr. Turner and deliver it back to him."

Hank Fisher rubbed his mustache like it itched something terrible. His eyes narrowed as if he were trying to make a decision. "George, I guess you're old enough to know this, so I'll tell you straight. Wild Tom Turner is a lot worse than Thorne. Stay away from him. Let Thorne run his own errands. The medicine that Thorne wants is alcohol."

I figured as much. I knew this was not something I should do for Thorne. On the other hand, if he was going to drink anyway, maybe it wouldn't hurt anything for me to help him out, particularly if doing so might bring Tucker back to me.

Doubting that Mr. Fisher understood my dilemma and what was at stake, I climbed back onto the maintainer and continued my work, trying as best I could to put Thorne's demands out of my head.

A boy driving a maintainer loaded with food and supplies must have been a strange sight, but each house where I stopped held friendly and grateful people who somehow knew me even though I did not know them. Invariably, they asked about their neighbors and wanted to know if there was anything they could do to help me or anyone else.

As the day progressed, I was reminded that the citizens of Cherokee County were one of a kind—generous, compassionate, and self-sacrificing. I was proud to be one of them, and I knew it would be hard to leave this community —my community—behind. I pushed Minnesota out of my head again, as I had done so many times in the last few weeks, and wondered at the number of people who wanted to lend a hand to their neighbors. Many offered to take a turn on the maintainer, but I knew that things would have to get much worse before Grandpa would accept help from anyone who wasn't a McCray.

Many folks, hardy as they were, seemed frightened by the extreme weather. For some, my grandfather and I were the only contact they had with the outside world that week. Whether friend or stranger, they all wanted news and information, but most of all they wanted Grandpa and me to know how much they appreciated what we were doing for them. Several commented that it was so quiet without television, radio, or phones and that all they had heard for days now was wind and snow blowing up against their windows —that, and the welcome sound of the giant maintainer in their driveway.

As I did my work, trying to properly grade the road, thoughts of Thorne and his proposition turned over in my mind, though Mr. Fisher's reaction gave me second thoughts. Still, what harm would it do if I got a couple of bottles for Thorne? If I didn't, he would find someone else to get them for him. If I did, maybe I could get Tucker back.

On this, my third full day on the job, I worked straight through lunch, pulling off bits of my sandwich as I watched the road, and by 3:00 that afternoon, I was a little ahead of schedule.

If I went west six miles and two miles north to Crossing Trails, maybe I could get the road cleared for the dairy truck, but there was Mrs. Slater to worry about, so I decided not to risk it. She lived to the east, so I headed the maintainer in her direction, pushing snow out of the way as I went.

I had my eyes open, wondering if fate might put Tom Turner in my path. Like most people looking for trouble, I quickly learned that it is seldom hard to find.

There was no answer when I knocked on Mrs. Slater's door, and I wondered if she was staying with neighbors. After knocking again and waiting, I circled around the house and tried to look in some windows. I could see Mrs. Slater, who lived alone, lying on her sofa. Considering the medicine more important than her nap, I rapped on the window. She stirred and turned her head to the noise but didn't get up, so I rapped again. She looked confused.

I went around to the back door, which was unlocked. I stepped inside.

"Mrs. Slater. It's George McCray. I have your medicine."

"Please come here." Her voice was weak, like she was sick.

I found Mrs. Slater perspiring despite the cold, and a little shaky.

"Do you have my insulin?"

Digging into my pocket, I gave her the small glass vials. "Yes, right here."

"Thank goodness you made it. I was all out."

After inoculating herself, she said she was feeling better. I went out to the maintainer and

133

brought her back some milk and other groceries and promised that either my grandfather or I would look in on her again soon. She gave me a big hug and just would not stop thanking me.

As I made my way home on the maintainer, coming from the other direction, I noticed an overturned mailbox sticking out of the snow and a remnant of a driveway—more of a dirt trail and one I'd never noticed before. Then I saw the black lettering on the mailbox, U R N E R. This was it. A long lane wandered off the county road and up a hill covered in timber and brush. I was to clear all the driveways and this looked like a driveway to me. I backed up the maintainer and slowly climbed Blackberry Hill, moving snow as I went.

Chapter 23

At the top of a hill was a trailer, set amid a tangle of steel barrels, tires, and junky-looking car fenders protruding from beneath the deep snow in the front yard. I turned the maintainer around and sat for a second, trying to get up my nerve to either get out and go to the door or just put the maintainer in second and head back down the hill. Before I could decide, an old man came banging out the door, two scrawny black-and-tan coon dogs on his heels. Wild Tom Turner wore filthy jeans and cowboy boots, and spat brown tobacco juice into the white snow.

As he approached, I turned the engine down to idle and opened the door of the maintainer, staying put in the cab. He looked up at me, as if he were sizing me up.

"My name is George McCray. My grandfather asked me to check in and make sure you were all right. If you need food, I've got milk and groceries to tide you over."

He smiled shrewdly, flashing yellow-stained teeth, seemingly pleased to be getting something for free. "Neighborly of you, son."

"Also, wanted to ask if you could stay off the

roads for the rest of today and tomorrow. We're going to try to clear one lane first for emergency traffic. We'll come back and do the other lane later."

"I'm not going anywhere in particular."

"Thanks." I paused, trying to muster the courage to ask for what Thorne wanted.

"So, you're Big Bo McCray's son?"

"Grandson," I corrected.

He nodded his head approvingly and said, "I'll take some milk if you're giving it away."

I reached back and gave him two bottles. He took them and started back to the trailer.

"Wait," I called after him. "You're Mr. Turner, right?"

He turned and spat again. "What of it?"

"My grandfather also said that if you had anything extra you could share with neighbors that I should get that, too."

"What kind of 'extras' did your grandfather have in mind?"

"Mostly food, but if you've got an extra lantern or kindling . . ." I hesitated and tried to add my next request like an afterthought. "Also, Mr. Thorne, our neighbor, he's been sick and he said if I came by this way that I should ask you for, uh, two bottles of your best medicine."

He smiled in a way that made me uncomfortable. "So, Frank drank up all his own and he can't get to the pharmacy in town for more, eh?

136

Wait here." Turner disappeared inside his trailer and came out with two mayonnaise jars filled with a muddy brown liquid. He handed them to me, chuckled, and said, "You tell Mr. Thorne that he should take two cups every night before he goes to bed, and I'll be sending him my doctor bill."

I nestled the jars inside my extra coat so the liquid would not spill. "Thanks, Mr. Turner. I'll tell him."

"Listen, son, this business is between me and Mr. Thorne." A vicious look crept across his face. "No one else need know, you understand?"

"Yes, sir, I understand."

"Good. Now you get back to your work and I'll get back to mine." He gave a halfhearted wave as he turned around and went back to his trailer, the dogs following.

As I made my way down off of Blackberry Hill, that cold sweat was back, along with an uncomfortable knot in my stomach.

Plowing the roads toward home, I had no idea what to do. I contemplated emptying the jars, but it occurred to me that I had already done the hard part. All I had to do now was give them to Thorne and take back Tucker. Everyone would be better off. I would have what I wanted. Thorne would have what he wanted. Tucker would have a decent home.

When I returned to the farm that evening, I

137

hid the jars in the implement shed before Grandpa and I milked again. I was quiet and my grandfather worried about me.

"You tired?"

"Yes," I answered.

He looked at me and nodded his head up and down approvingly. "That's okay." He turned and walked off, climbed onto the maintainer, and was off for the nighttime shift.

While he went off to work, I went into the living room. Behind the puzzle table where my grandmother and father had spent so many hours stood a bookcase with leaded-glass doors. My dad proudly displayed his encyclopedia on the top three shelves. I took down the first volume, sat in Grandpa's recliner, and started to read about alcoholism in the dim light of the kerosene lamp that I rested on the puzzle table. More than halfway through the entry, I realized that my grandmother was standing beside the chair, at my shoulder.

"Catching up on some schoolwork?"

I slammed the book shut and tried to act casual. "No, just something I was interested in."

"Okay, but you better get to sleep. Your shift will begin soon."

I replaced the volume on the shelf, brushed my teeth, and went to bed, still uncertain of how I would handle Thorne.

Chapter 24

"George!" Grandma yelled up the stairs. "Time to get up!" Every morning, as my fatigue built, it grew harder and harder to wake up. I could hear the maintainer idling in the driveway. It had been running nonstop for four days straight and the roads were still a mess.

After a quick breakfast, I joined my grandfather in the barn to help him finish the morning milking. My mind quickly went to the jars in the implement shed, and I felt a queasy mixture of nerves and shame brewing inside of me.

"Grandpa, Frank Thorne is sick," I blurted out. This was my guilt talking. I hadn't intended to bring up the object of my anxiety, but a part of me hungered for some direction. "I think he has the flu, or it could be tremors. His house is cold. He needs wood."

"That's kind of you to be concerned."

"Actually, I was thinking more about Tucker than Thorne." This was partly true, but I was still on a fishing expedition, hoping for some kind of sign from Grandpa Bo that would send me in one direction or another.

"We've got plenty of wood. I'll put some on

the steel shelf behind the cab and you can unload it on your way out." I started out the barn door, excited to see Tucker and now feeling less guilty since Grandpa had given me a legitimate reason to stop at Thorne's. "Don't forget to crack the ice on the pond before you leave," he reminded me.

By the time I got out of our driveway and into Thorne's, even though I had been working for hours, it was still early in the morning and I did not want to wake him. Tucker watched me from the door, tail wagging, as I unloaded the wood onto the small front porch. I thought of the mayonnaise jars that I'd snuck back into the cab, but I didn't want to leave them out in plain sight with the wood. I considered slipping them through the perpetually unlocked front door, but I was afraid I'd cause a ruckus with Tucker and disturb Thorne. I would come back later to finish what I'd started. I glanced through the door at the big red dog, his eyes full of expectation.

"I'll be back for you later, Tucker," I said softly before I set out on my shift.

When I got to the far eastern edge of our clearing territory, I stopped and checked in with the Sloan family.

Mr. Sloan had a new job for me. The mailman had left all of the mail for our section of the county with the Sloans because it was impossible for him to get down most of the roads. I picked up mail for the roads that were on our route and promised to distribute it as best I could. There was another letter from Minnesota addressed to me from my mother. I stuck it in my coat pocket to read when I had time.

By 4:00 that afternoon, my shift was ending and I was heading west. I slowed the maintainer and considered whether or not I should stop at Thorne's. My resolve to finish my "errand" was suddenly less firm, the guilt creeping back in to fill the void. Still, I wanted to check on Tucker, and unfortunately, there was no way to separate him from Thorne. All day long, the jars had been buried beneath my extra coat, and I had wanted to get rid of them. Now, as I plowed up Thorne's driveway and put the maintainer into idle, I decided to leave them in their hiding place.

There were considerable footsteps and paw prints in the snow, but Thorne's truck was still parked in the same place. A good bit of the firewood I'd left on the porch had been taken. Before I even knocked, Tucker was at the front door, pawing anxiously for me to let him out.

"Mr. Thorne, it's George," I called.

"Come in, boy."

I pushed the door open and stepped inside. Everything was so different that I was disoriented. The inside had gone through the most amazing transformation I had ever seen. The curtains were pulled back, the windows cleaned so that light cascaded into what now seemed more like a cozy cabin than a broken-down shack. The place was spotless. Though the house was still without power, a fire burned warm and full in the stove, and I could smell soup simmering and cornbread in the oven. The floors were clean, the clutter and garbage gone. Thorne was still on the sofa, but he was wearing clean clothes and was shaven.

Tucker whined. "Let the dog out, would you, son?"

"Sure." As I did so, I tried to take in the transformation. I looked at the wall of photos. Something else was different. The picture was gone. For some reason, he had taken it down.

Thorne looked so much better. I was pondering what had brought this about when he got down to the business I was dreading.

"Did you bring me the medicine?"

It wasn't medicine. It was poison. However much it might have gotten me what I wanted, I knew that even Thorne deserved better. "No, I didn't," I lied, mustering my strength. "That's not the kind of medicine you need, Mr. Thorne."

He grimaced. But what he said next surprised me.

"Good. You're a pretty smart kid, aren't you? Just like your dad."

I didn't know how to answer.

"It's not something I should have asked you

to do." He smiled. "But I do have another favor to ask, and this one won't bother you. My dog is tired of being all cooped up. Why don't you take him with you while you're working on that maintainer? He loves to go for a ride. All he does is sit around here and whine to go outside. Can you do that for me?"

"Yes, sir. I could do that." I struggled to control my excitement, but inside I wanted to pop.

"Good. Now, you get on home before your grandparents start worrying about you. Frank Thorne will be fine."

I went out the door and bent down, allowing Tucker to nuzzle his cold snout into my face. "As soon as this snow lets up, you and I are going romping again! And in the meantime, you can come to work with me on snow days." I pulled him close, knowing that I'd made the right choice, for Frank Thorne and for myself. I held the dog tight to me for a few more moments before I opened the door and put him back in the house.

The maintainer climbed up McCray's Hill, grading all the while. As soon as I parked, I carefully carried what I'd hidden in the cab to the back of the barnyard, out of sight of the house. I opened the mayonnaise jars and poured Turner's homemade rotgut into the snow, hiding the empties at the bottom of the trash cans we kept behind the barn.

With the crime scene neatened up, and no discernable scent of alcohol lingering in the cold, clean air, I ran up to the house to give my grandmother the good news about Tucker. When I opened the door, a familiar aroma confused me, until I put the pieces together. On the table was fresh-baked cornbread. My grandmother stood at the stove, stirring a big kettle of her bean soup. These were the smells in Thorne's cabin.

"Grandma," I said, as I hugged her extra hard.

"What?" she asked.

"Oh, nothing."

She smiled and went back to work and I just watched her busying herself. No one else in our family would ever know how or where she spent that particular day. The idea of angels is appealing to me. Whether they exist or not, I can't say. I do know that some people are called on to do good deeds. Grandma Cora was the closest thing to an angel I ever knew. It was not lost on me how our days had differed when it came to Thorne. I had tried to take advantage of his illness to get what I wanted; she was trying to support his recovery.

My grandfather and I worked the maintainer in shifts for the next three days and nights, Tucker at my side to keep me company. At first, he was a little reluctant about jumping into the cab, but after a little coaxing he was right at home. I made a bed for him behind the seat from old blankets and coats. Having Tucker with me made the work seem more tolerable and the hours passed by quickly. From time to time, I imagined he would shout up little commands to make sure I was paying attention. "Look out there, George, you're drifting to the right."

I let him know who was boss. "You can't even walk a straight line, Tucker. So don't tell me how to plow!"

The snow let up, but the real problem was the wind, which caused drifts into the roadway so that we were having to redo what we had previously done. Still, we made progress, having cleared all of the main roads and shifting to the more isolated side roads and country lanes.

We were exhausted, but the winds were dying down and we were gaining ground. The dairy truck was coming again, and both the power and phone companies were able to start making repairs. The temperature was also climbing, and as we thawed out from the big storm, things were getting back to normal. Soon, McCray's Dairy had power and phone service, and the worst was behind us.

There were only a few days of school left before the Christmas break and I was hoping that all the canceled days would mean a free pass for me on both algebra and memorizing lines for the school play.

My grandfather gave me ten dollars and suggested that I do some Christmas shopping with my grandma—at least as soon as I cracked the ice and did the milking.

The next morning, Grandma and I decided we needed rest, so shopping would wait another day. After breakfast, I re-read the letter from my mom that I had stashed very carefully in my pocket. She said that they would be driving to Kansas and hoping to arrive no later than December 24, roads allowing. She said that I should be packed and ready to go by December 27. School started in Minnesota on January 5. I tossed the letter aside and tried not to think about it.

Chapter 25

On December 19, my second day off in a row, I took Tucker for a long walk. It seemed that Frank Thorne's health was continuing to improve. When I brought Tucker back, Thorne even asked me to come inside and sit down. I did not have much to say, so after a few awkward moments, I said my goodbyes and headed home.

Grandma made a huge lunch and I must have eaten too much. I felt exhausted, so I stretched out on my bed for what I thought would be a short nap before I helped with the afternoon milking. I did not wake up until 7:30 the next morning.

Stumbling out of bed, embarrassed, I wondered why no one had woken me. Downstairs, both of my grandparents were very quiet, probably a bit irritated at me for sleeping in and not helping with the chores, I thought.

It was up to me to make some conversation. "I better go check the pond and clear the ice."

My grandfather barely looked up. "Thanks, you do that."

It went quiet again, and I ate in silence until my grandfather spoke.

"George, I took the trash down to the dump and I pulled out two empty jars that looked strange to me. You probably think that I'm too old to have noticed, but there had been alcohol in them."

As I gulped the last of my oatmeal, I'm sure my face turned as white as the snow I had been plowing.

"Do you have any idea how those jars got in the trash?"

Rising from the table and pulling on my coat, I planned to toss a quick "don't know" over my shoulder and head out.

"George, get back over here and sit down."

I sighed, knowing I'd have to tell them everything, wondering if they'd understand. "Yes, I know how they got there, but it's not what you think."

"Try me," my grandfather said.

I told them the whole story. My grandmother had her hands on her hips, her irritation with me slowly dissipating. Grandpa Bo listened with an impassive look on his face, until he cracked a bemused smile and spoke.

"Well, can we agree that'll be your first and last trip up to Blackberry Hill?"

"Yes, sir."

"I'm disappointed that you chose to run that errand for Thorne, incomplete as it was, but I'm proud of you for one thing."

"What's that, Grandpa?"

"You were able to correct your course after you made a wrong turn. That's a good skill for a maintainer. Now get on out of here and crack the ice."

Not until I had my own children did I realize how skillful my grandparents were at parenting. It is extraordinarily difficult to simultaneously correct and support a teenager. They actually made me feel better about myself and them when I made mistakes. My misjudgments and wrong turns were opportunities to learn from and not events to be ashamed of.

Walking out the door to crack the ice, I realized I had no idea how I was going to say goodbye to two such wonderful people, whom I loved to the core. What would life be like without them?

When I got to the pond, I discovered there was no need to chop the ice. It had grown so warm, almost fifty degrees the day before, that the opening had not frozen over. The cows were ambling down to the lake for a drink and the heifers were bawling for their mothers. There was a strange smell in the air—at least for that time of year. I looked to the sky to confirm what I thought.

Snow clouds are a light gray color and just reach right down to the trees so that the spaces between the sky and the land all come together without dramatic contrasts. The sky that morning was very different. Overhead it was clear and bright and to the east the sun was giving us everything she had to give. But to the west, the sky was black as night and I could hear thunder booming on the horizon. I smelled rain. Thunderstorms were for spring and summer, not winter. This made no sense to me.

Although I might have recalled occasional lightning strikes, I could not remember ever seeing a winter thunderstorm.

I went up to the dairy barn to help my grandfather finish the milking and ask about the weather.

"Grandpa, have you seen the sky to the west?"

"I sure have and I've listened to the weather report, too."

"What's it doing?"

He grunted. "It's not good."

"What do you mean?"

"George, you've done a good job helping us dig out of two feet of snow and now you just might find out what's ten times worse than snow for a road maintainer—ice."

"Ice?"

"I'll take a foot of snow over an inch of freezing rain any day. Freezing rain coats every piece of gravel and every tree limb. The maintainer's tires can't get enough traction to do any work. On top of that, after an inch or so of freezing rain, branches, limbs, and eventually entire trees will crumble under the weight of the ice. Falling timber will block the roads and the power lines will be ripped straight off the poles. It's a maintainer's nightmare. We could be down for weeks."

"What can we do?"

"Nothing, son. Nothing at all."

My grandfather and the local weather forecasters thought we were going to pay the price for the warm air that had blessed us the last few days. A cold front had marched down from the north and was prepared to do battle with the warm air that still lingered from the south, and just like it was during the Civil War, Kansas was stuck right in the middle. Thirty miles to the north, it would be several degrees colder. They would get snow—to be pushed aside with minimal difficulties. Thirty miles to the south it would be a few degrees warmer and they would get a cold but harmless rain. Stuck right in the middle, we would get paralyzing ice.

By 2:00 P.M. on December 20, 1962, the freezing rain hit, dumping a little over an inch of hard frozen ice on the road. It was a mess, just as forecast.

However bad it might have been for the roads and the trees, it was beautiful outside. The ice coated everything and made the whole world glisten and shine. It was as if the universe were flash-frozen, leaving all life suspended.

It could be weeks before we thawed out.

Anything that could get wet was also now coated in ice: trees, buildings, horses, cows, sheep, rocks, and, worst of all for us, roads.

Cherokee County, Kansas, ground to a total halt.

While I knew what a mess snow would cause, I had no idea what damage a solid inch of ice could do. I hoped that people had learned their lesson and had stocked plenty of supplies in the few days we had between storms. We were in for a very tough week leading up to Christmas and probably into the New Year.

We did not even bother starting the maintainer. My grandfather and I cracked the ice on the pond, milked the cows by hand, and dumped the milk on the ground, and we all went to bed early, not knowing what the coming days would bring.

Chapter 26

It was less than a week away and the prospect of a decent Christmas was fading fast. My scheme to get Tucker back was not working. We had no power and the phone lines were down. I had not talked to my mom or sisters in over a week. While hoping that the weather and the road conditions would improve, I was left wondering if they would be able to make it through the final thirty miles of the trip home, where the snow had turned to ice.

The tree I had cut for Grandma Cora had made it as far as the tree stand in the living room, but we'd been so busy with snow days that it had sat, undecorated, for all this time. Just like our milk, it seemed like the holiday was going to be thrown out. I was trying to act like I didn't care, but it was hard to give up on Christmas.

Lying in bed that night, I could hear tree limbs creak and moan under the weight of the ice. This storm was bad for us, but for some of our neighbors it had to be worse. Mrs. Slater needed her insulin, Sherry Rather had her baby to deliver, and old Mrs. Reed would be worried sick. Most everyone was frightened and here I was just lying in bed doing nothing. It left me feeling rather useless and sick to my stomach.

I wondered if we should just walk the frozen roads of Cherokee County. Maybe we couldn't maintain the roads, but we might still be able to help the people who lived along them.

The next morning I brought up my idea.

"Grandpa, maybe we should check on some of our neighbors and make sure they aren't hurt or in need of anything."

He looked at me, equally disgusted by the whole situation. "There is just not much we can do."

My grandmother reached out and patted my arm. "It's nice of you to think of them."

"But how about Mrs. Slater and old Mrs. Reed and the people who aren't so healthy?"

"They have good neighbors that live much closer than we do. In this ice, a person would be lucky to walk a mile an hour. Mrs. Slater lives eight miles from here. It might take you eight hours to just get there and another eight to walk home. What could you do if she did need help?"

"I guess you're right, but it just doesn't seem right to sit and do nothing."

My grandfather didn't say anything. My grandmother looked bothered, too, but she seemed to accept there was little we could do. "We're hoping the weather will warm again in a few days and we can melt our way out of the ice."

"Well, what if it doesn't? Christmas will be

over. How will Mom and the girls make it here?"

"We'll still have Christmas, George. A lot can happen in a few days. You'll see."

After breakfast, my grandfather started up the chain saw and began clearing our yard of the branches and limbs that had cracked and fallen to the ground from the weight of the ice. I was out helping him in the yard when the back door opened and Grandma called, "George, come up to the house."

She was waiting for me at the back door with two plates full of warm food, covered in aluminum foil. "Just the man I was looking for."

I eyed her suspiciously. "What?"

"I need a delivery. Top plate to Frank Thorne and the bottom plate is for a red dog, but don't stay too long; lunch is almost ready and your grandpa promised me I could have you to myself this afternoon. We have some Christmas work to do."

I took the plates away from her. "Sure, I can take them!"

Once out of her view, I stopped and peeked under the foil. Thorne's plate had several pieces of cornbread and the remaining space was filled with fresh-out-of-the-oven Christmas cookies— cut into the shapes of trees and snowmen that were colored red and green and covered with sprinkles. Tucker's plate had a soup bone with plenty of meat carelessly left attached. I shuffled down the icy road, trying not to fall and spill the food, smiling most of the way.

As I suspected, both Thorne and Tucker were pleased by my delivery, and playing the role of Santa improved my spirits, too. The soup bone was a big hit and Tucker immediately went to work on it.

When I got ready to return, Thorne put his hand on my shoulder. "Why don't you come around tomorrow, too, when you can stay longer. Maybe, if it's a little nicer out, you can take him for a walk."

I reached down and gave Tucker a farewell hug. "I'd like that."

Tearing himself away from his treat, Tucker looked at me gratefully and seemed to say, "That'll work, but could you bring another bone, too?"

The lunch menu that afternoon was exactly what I expected: soup, cornbread, and Christmas cookies. As soon as we had the dishes cleaned and put away, my grandmother and I carried up boxes of decorations from the basement and we finally attended to the tree I had dragged from the creek.

We put lights on it and I hung what was left of the cookies that she had baked for Frank Thorne, as well as all the decorations from past McCray Christmases. As I handled the old ornaments, it was easy to let my mind drift back to happier times, when we'd all been together. Grandma Cora had grown quiet, too, and I'm sure she felt the same odd mix of melancholy and forced holiday cheer that was taking hold of me.

It was too early to start making new Christmas memories, it seemed, but I didn't want my grandmother to slip back into sadness, thinking of her lost son. There seemed to be a few extra cookies and the kid in me took over, once again. When my grandmother wasn't looking, I would pop them into my mouth and quickly chew and swallow them, another McCray tradition.

"Something seems to be getting into our cookies," Grandma announced.

"How can you tell?"

She reached out with her thumb and touched my cheeks. "He's got green crumbs all over his face, and he's got the same silly grin on his face his dad used to get."

I smiled even bigger, and I think we were both glad to have acknowledged my father, even in this small way. By doing so, it was as if we could now allow ourselves to have a little fun decorating the tree.

When we were finished, Grandma plugged in the lights and, with the power out, they did not come on. She shrugged her shoulders and said, "I guess that pretty much sums up our year, doesn't it, George." I am sure at that moment that neither of us knew whether to laugh or to cry.

Chapter 27

The next morning, I knocked on Thorne's door and he tossed out a friendly "Come in."

The little house was still reasonably clean and warm, and Thorne was busily tinkering with a carburetor that rested on the kitchen table. He pointed to a leash that hung by the door, knowing precisely why I was there. "Take the leash and be careful. It's pretty slick out there."

I snapped the leash on Tucker's collar and we headed out the door. "Thanks, Mr. Thorne. I'll bring him back in a few hours."

It felt good to have Tucker walking beside me. We made our way to Mack's Lake and knocked around his old cabin, but it was too cold to stay out for long, so after we took in our frozen surroundings we headed back to civilization.

We were living atop a polar ice cap that had hills and crystallized trees pushing up through the ice like statues protruding from stone ruins. With four legs, Tucker moved through the glassy terrain easier than I could, but still he had to be careful. With so little traction, I slipped around and could not get my footing.

There was the eerie sound of tree branches

cracking and snapping all around us, like distant cannon fire. Periodically, giant crashing noises came from the forest that flanked Kill Creek. Ancient tree trunks snapped under the weight of the ice and fell to the ground with thuds that echoed for miles along the riverbank. Tucker and I steered clear of the tree cover as we walked toward our farm.

My grandfather had worked all day with his chain saw, trying to clear the yard of branches and debris, and he still had a lot more to do. Tucker followed me around for an hour or so while I tried to stack the logs and branches that Grandpa had cut out of the way. There would be plenty of firewood for years to come.

After two weeks of being the first assistant to the Senior Road Maintainer, I naturally thought of my job. I walked to the end of the driveway and looked in both directions to see a tangled mess of ice and fallen debris. Eventually, I took Tucker back to Thorne's cabin. Thorne was still intently working on his project, so I said a quick goodbye to Tucker and just released him inside the door. As I headed home, I grew a little gloomy. It was hard to think of Tucker like a neighbor friend whom I could walk with from time to time but not do much else with.

All of these snow days were also making me miss my friends. I wanted my normal routine back, even if it meant going to school.

The time I had left in Cherokee County was running out with each passing day. As best I could, I tried to accept that this was the way things had to be.

When I got home, my grandfather stopped his cutting and we did the milking together. For yet another day, our cows' efforts were ultimately poured on the ground. We started inside for dinner and I wondered aloud why we could not at least make some effort to beat this weather.

"Grandpa, I want to start up the maintainer and give it a try. It doesn't feel right doing nothing."

"George, you've never tried to drive a maintainer on ice. It can handle a half inch, but a whole inch of ice is too much. You're going to have to trust me; it can't be done. You'll slip all over the place."

I dug my heels in. "I want to try."

He turned and walked away. "Suit yourself."

After I warmed the diesel engine, it turned right over, sputtering, and then it evened out. With very little light left, I put the maintainer in reverse and eased slowly out the barn door. The weight of the maintainer cracked through the ice and reached the solid frozen grass beneath me. There was enough traction to back straight out. Encouraged, I moved through the barnyard and to the entrance of our gravel driveway without slipping around too much. Slowly lowering the blade, I tried to inch forward and turn over the gravel. The second the blade hit the ice, the resistance caused the machine to lose traction, and my wheels started to spin.

Backing up, I tried again at several different speeds and blade angles. Same result. Sitting there in the cab, I could hardly stand it. My own anger and frustration started to build. Backing the machine up, I got a good running start. When I had built up enough momentum, I dropped the blade violently, hoping to crack the icy surface. The maintainer spun hard and rocked up into the yard, where I had no business being. When I tried to back out, the maintainer's tires spun.

I was stuck. Reversing didn't work, either.

Knowing my grandfather would be unhappy with me, I started to feel very foolish.

He walked out the back door, right past me, without saying a word.

Not knowing what else to do, I just sat and waited. Soon I heard the sound of the big International Harvester tractor coming toward me in the last light of the day. He parked the tractor pointing downhill from the maintainer, where he would have more traction, and then got out of the cab and connected the tractor to the grader with a long chain. The tractor's tires were twice the size of the maintainer's, so it had much better pulling power. Still, there was no guarantee he could pull me out.

My grandfather walked up to the cab door.

When I opened it, he didn't appear mad. In fact, he just smiled and said, "Can't grade in the ice, George." Apparently, Big Bo McCray had passed some of his legendary stubborn streak onto his grandson.

For once, it was me who didn't say a word.

"Put the transmission in reverse. When the chain is taut, let out the clutch slowly. I'll try to pull you to level ground. Let's hope we don't both get stuck."

It took us several tries before he was able to get me pulled back to a flatter area where the maintainer's wheels didn't just spin. Maybe it was because I didn't know better, but I didn't want to give up.

After we had both implements back in the barn, I got my nerve up to keep pushing. "Grandpa, why can't we hook up Dick and Dock, like you used to before you got the maintainer, and try to grade the old-fashioned way?"

"George, Dick and Dock are twice as old as me in horse years. They'd barely make it down the driveway before they dug in their heels and turned back to their warm stalls. And what if one of them slipped and broke a leg?"

"Well, don't we use chains on the car tires sometimes? Couldn't we put chains on the maintainer, too?"

"They don't make chains that big. Besides, with ice this thick, I doubt chains would make a difference. A car just has to push itself forward; a maintainer has a much harder job. It has to move itself forward and scrape thousands of pounds of ice off the road at the same time. That takes traction, and lots of it."

"There just has to be some way."

My grandfather looked pained. It didn't occur to me that this was bothering him just as much as or more than it was bothering me. "Why don't you go inside and let me think about it. Sometimes we just have to accept that there are things we can't fix. Things are not always the way we want them . . ."

His words trailed off and I heard something I didn't think was possible. There were no tears in the eyes of Big Bo McCray, but there was a pained break in his voice that probably surprised him as much as it did me. I walked over to my grandfather and put my arms around him. He gave me a big hug. "I'm sorry, George. None of us like to feel helpless."

He squeezed me a little tighter and for a moment it felt very much like I had a father again. He released his grip and turned and walked away. Walking back to the house, I felt a little sorry for the way I had behaved.

By the time I got back inside the kitchen, it was dark out and Grandma had lit the kerosene lamp. My grandfather did not come up to the house for dinner.

At first, Grandma did not seem that worried. She just left his plate of food covered in the oven and we ate without him. By 7:15, when there was still no sign of him, she began nervously looking out the back door.

"Do you want me check on him, Grandma?"

"No, I'm sure he's fine. It's just not like him to stay out so late."

A little past 7:30 that night, we heard the maintainer engine turn over.

"What is he up to out there?" my grandmother asked.

The maintainer eased out of the barn and turned into the driveway and stopped. The light from the headlamps reflected off branches encased in glass. The cab door swung open and my grandfather came up to the back porch. I did not realize why at the time, but he moved sure-footedly on the ice.

Grandma pushed open the back door and called out to him.

"Get inside, Bo! It's late!"

But he made no move to come into the house and just looked at her.

"What is it, Bo?"

"Maybe I'm a fool, Cora, but George is right. People are counting on us. There is something I want to try. It just might work. Don't wait up for me; I'll be back when I'm finished."

"Bo, you can't go out in this ice. You and

George couldn't even get out of the driveway. This is crazy. Where are you going?"

"It'll be fine. I've got it all worked out." He turned and headed back to the maintainer, climbing into the cab and releasing the brake. I watched silently as he headed down the driveway at a snail's pace.

Grandma was furious. She paced about the kitchen for the rest of the evening, carrying on an angry monologue under her breath, and eventually she went to bed early without saying goodnight.

With the exclusive use of the kerosene lamp, I wandered into my parents' room and looked around. It seemed that I had been avoiding this room for many months now.

There were still pictures of my dad on the bed-side table and on the wall along with the other family photos. This room had been his when he was a boy and the same dresser had stayed in there all of these years. I opened some of the drawers in the chest. There were four or five worn-down pencils, some firecrackers he had taken away from me, change, ticket stubs, and the yellow pocketknife, with a bone handle, that I gave him for Christmas. A strong feeling came over me that my dad would want me to have that knife, that somehow it was rightfully mine. I slipped it into my pocket and held it close. It felt good to have something on me that connected us.

There was no reason for me to sleep upstairs where it was so cold and leave Grandma downstairs by herself, so I just climbed into the double bed. It seemed luxurious having that giant bed all to myself. It would have been even better with a big, furry, red pillow, even if it did tend to wiggle and lick my face. Reading by the dim light of the lamp, I quickly felt drowsy, so I turned it off and listened to the wind blowing against the window. The iced-over branches sounded like wind chimes knocking up against the house. While wondering what my grandfather was up to, I drifted off to sleep.

Chapter 28

It was light out when I woke up. It had been a long, snug, and secure sleep, but I wondered why no one had bothered to wake me. I threw off the covers and raced into the kitchen. My grandmother was standing over the sink, looking out the kitchen window. "What's wrong, Grandma?"

"Your grandfather still hasn't come back and I am worried."

"Don't worry, Grandma. He'll be all right." While I could tell my grandmother not to worry, I wasn't so good at following my own advice. I couldn't imagine where he was and was hoping he had not slipped off the road in the middle of the night, or worse. Pushing him the way I had to do something about the roads made me feel responsible.

We ate breakfast in silence. Perhaps because I just wanted to stay busy, I went straight to the chores. And since I got such a late start, I did the milking first and figured I would chop the pond ice later. After letting in the first six cattle, I milked as furiously as I could, working up a sweat despite the cold. The whole time my worry climbed and my mind raced to terrible possibilities. Why had he not told us where he was going or what he was doing? I didn't even know where to look. The milking seemed to take forever.

Finally, I got to the last six cows. When finished, I shut the barn door, closed the latch, and ran to the house, hoping that there was some good news.

My grandmother was dressed in her winter coat and was standing by the back door. "Where are you going?" I asked.

"I'm going out to find your grandfather."

"Now?"

"Yes."

"I'll go with you."

"No, you better stay here. In case he shows up, we can't all be roaming around trying to find him. I won't be gone more than an hour."

I didn't want her to go, but I knew I had no say in the matter. The door shut behind her and just like that I was left alone, more alone than you could imagine. It came to me that I had lost my father and because I lost my father, I lost my mother, albeit it to sadness, loneliness, and a move to Minnesota. She was alive but she was absent from my life. Now my grandfather was lost and that meant my grandmother would wander about in freezing weather looking for him. Losses compound and impact us like falling dominoes. It was just me—alone in the old farmhouse listening to the wind shake our house down to its foundation.

I pictured my grandparents pushing against the snow, determined to find each other. Needing to get my mind separated from my worry, I tried to read, but it was no use. I should have insisted that I go with her, but I was thirteen and generally did what I was told. We could have left a note. There was some solace in remembering how strong she was when we searched for the Christmas tree. I paced about the house and tried to formulate a plan of my own. When more than an hour had passed and still no one had returned, I reassured myself that she probably did not have a watch and when she said an hour it was only an estimate.

When she got back, I would bundle up and go in the opposite direction. We could take turns like that, one-hour shifts each. I searched around for the heaviest winter clothes I could find and arranged them around the periphery of the downstairs furnace grate. As soon as she returned, I'd dress in my pre-warmed things and go out. I thought about survival. If I got lost I would need food. I placed a few apples and some cookies in a knapsack and went to the basement and dug up an old army canteen that had belonged to Dad.

Back in the kitchen, I took a drink from my grandfather's tin cup, which so reminded me of him, and then pressed my face against the cold window. I peered outside and into the ice-land of meadows to the south of our old home, hoping for some sign of my grandparents' return. Amid all of the worrying, a sickening realization came over me. I had forgotten to clear the ice on the pond for the cows.

Quickly, I pulled on my warm winter suit and headed out the door.

Chapter 29

The faster I tried to go, the more I slipped and fell, which only caused me to worry more about my grandparents. It was hard going forward when the elevation increased and nearly impossible to stop sliding on the downhill sections. Fortunately, our farm sat on the top of a hill, and at least for the first several minutes, I could move across the barnyard using a skating motion.

Not wanting to take the time to skate over to the open gate, I squeezed my way between the strands of the barbed-wire fence that separates the barn pasture from the lake meadow. My extra clothing added to my girth and my jacket caught on one of the small barbs. Backing out, I reached around and pulled the fabric from the barb and tried again.

Once through the fence, I slid to the bottom of the hill and tried to make my way up the back side of the pond, where a dam held the water back. It was too steep to go over, so I followed the dam around to the east of the pond. As I made my way around the spillway, where the water overflows in strong spring showers, my heart sank.

Forty feet from the shoreline, two cows and two calves had wandered out onto the ice and fallen through a weak spot. They were treading water as best they could. One calf was barely holding his head above water. The remainder of the herd stood precariously close, tempting their own fate. Nausea and panic came over me in waves. There was no one home to help me. My grandfather's words came back to me. "It's an important job I'm giving you. Do you under-stand?"

How casually I had said, "Sure."

Now I needed help, and a lot of it. I yelled as loud as I could. "Help!" My voice echoed over the hills and valleys and cruelly reverberated off the ice-covered ground. Again, I was alone.

I wanted to stop right there and just sob at my helplessness. I wanted to jump in with them. Give up. At least that way, we would all go together. The sight of the first floating carcass snapped me to my senses. The poor creature's body bobbed up and down like a grotesque black-and-white ice cube. It was one of the two calves.

None of my options seemed reasonable. The cows weighed over twelve hundred pounds. I couldn't lift them up and onto the ice. From my daily efforts at cracking the ice with the sledge-hammer, I knew it would be impossible for me to clear a swath to the shore by hand.

There was only one way. I would have to pull them out one at a time with some rope and the tractor. Even though no one could hear me, I screamed again, as loud as I could. "Help!"

There was so little time. I ran across the ice back to the barn, driven by adrenaline and fear. More times than I could count, I fell. I got back up. I ran. I fell again.

First grabbing two ropes from the barn and a huge bucket of feed, I dashed to the implement shed and tried to remember how to start the largest tractor we owned, the IH. I had driven it many times, but I was so panicked that the simplest task seemed impossible. I had to try three times before the engine turned over and started. There was no time to let it warm up. I released the clutch with my numb feet and backed out of the barn. I swung the tractor forward and the massive wheels spun on the ice. Backing the throttle off, I tried again.

Eventually, I gained enough traction to move forward. Not wanting to waste an instant, I crashed through the gate, without bothering to open it, and made my way to the pond. The tractor would have to be pointing downhill when I tried to pull the cows out or it would not work. As I approached the pond, I picked the perfect spot, stopped the tractor, put it in reverse, and tried to get enough steam going to make it up a gentle hill that approached the west side of the pond. I had over fifty yards of lariat and I prayed it would reach.

Parking the tractor as close to the pond bank as possible, I quickly secured one end of the rope to the steel clevis on the back of the tractor. Pouring the sorghum on the shore worked exactly as I thought it would. The remainder of the herd that was not already in the water ambled over to the edge to eat, unaware that death was only twenty yards away.

With the bulk of the herd out of the way, I raced across the surface of the pond, holding on to the other end of the rope.

There was no time to think about it. Perhaps I should have known better than to risk my life for a few cows. But to me, they were living creatures with beating hearts that I had cared for my whole life, and that stood for our family's livelihood. I couldn't let them die without trying to rescue them. I knew full well it was more than cows I was trying to salvage.

I jumped. The cold water sucked the breath straight out of me. With the rope in my hand, I dove beneath the first cow. With hands frozen stiff, I managed to tie a knot around her. I tried to lift myself out of the ice but fell back in. My boots had filled with water and they were so heavy that they were pulling me down and making it hard to tread water. I kicked them off, but still I could not find a way out of the ice. A desperate cow's hoof slammed into me and I screamed out in pain. Now I was stuck, too.

I remembered the rope, somehow managed to grab it, and pulled myself out to safety.

Running and slipping across the surface of the pond in my stocking feet, my body a shivering, freezing mass of ice, I struggled up onto the tractor and pushed it into first gear. The right tractor wheel was spinning and the tractor could not gain traction. I backed up a little bit and tried again. Still, the right wheel spun. The tractor was set up with a right and a left brake pedal, so I tried to lock down the right wheel to transfer more of the pull to the left wheel. It worked. The tractor moved slowly forward, oblivious to its load. The rope went taut and pulled the cow up onto the ice. She plopped out onto the surface of the pond and let out a frightened bawl as I dragged her to the edge.

She came to her feet but was too frightened to let me get close enough to untie the knot. To make matters worse, the harder she pulled, the tighter it made the knot.

I didn't have time to wait for her to settle down. I remembered my father's pocketknife, pulled it out, and just cut the rope.

The rope was losing its flexibility in the cold. I backed the tractor to the edge of the pond. My feet were frozen. I jumped off the tractor and yanked the rope back to the edge of the water.

175

Holding on to the rope, I jumped in again. The water, being warmer than the outside air temperature and my frozen clothing, was not as bad this time, but still I felt like my blood was freezing. The other calf was the first animal I got to. He was struggling to get up onto the ice to follow the cow I had just retrieved, his mother. He seemed so small and helpless that I thought maybe I could pull him out by myself. Taking one end of the rope, I looped it around his backside, just under his tail, and then pulled myself up and out of the water. I was exhausted and frozen, and I questioned whether I had enough strength to pull out much more than a minnow from the frozen waters.

I'd lost my socks in the pond, too. The skin on the bottoms of my feet was wet and stuck to the surface of the ice. As much as it hurt, it also gave me traction. I yanked and pulled and cursed and screamed. The calf probably weighed close to two hundred pounds, but he was buoyant in the water. With him kicking and me pulling, he was able to work his front legs out of the water and onto the solid ice. With one final heave of everything I had left, the bawling calf slid out onto the surface of the ice. We lay there together on the ice for a moment, both of us panting, exhausted. Some skin had ripped from the bottom of my right foot and it began to bleed.

I was tired, so tired. I wanted to just lay there,

but I forced myself to my feet and untied the knot from the calf. There was one left. I stared at the water, ready to jump in. Perhaps I stood up too quickly, or perhaps it was fatigue, but the pond and ice started to swirl as if a giant tornado had uprooted me. I spun, turned, and fell to the ice with a thud. I could feel my eyelids flutter and I did not know what was wrong with me. I tried to fight my way back to consciousness, but everything was slipping away, getting darker and darker.

I don't know how much time passed, but something warm was licking my face. I tried to push it away and opened my eyes. Tucker was barking wildly. I tried to lift my hands to pull him close to me, but nothing would move. It went dark. Sleep. I had to sleep.

Then someone gripped me by the jacket and yanked me to my feet and began to drag me away from the ice. I remembered where I was and what I was doing and struggled to get loose. I yelled, "The cow!"

"Leave the damn cow," my rescuer swore, tossing me over his shoulder.

I shuddered convulsively in the clothing that was frozen to my body, my feet aching. I tried to resist. "We can't let her drown. . . ."

"Yes, we can."

With me resting on his shoulder like a sack of potatoes, Frank Thorne climbed onto the big

IH, slid the transmission into gear, and headed back to the house.

He pushed open the back door and carried me into the bathroom. He dropped me into the tub and immediately turned on the spigot, allowing life-giving warm water to pour over my frozen body.

Moments later my grandmother pushed open the back door and followed the trail of ice, snow, and mud into the bathroom. She took one look into the bathtub and screamed. Frank Thorne left before I could open my mouth to thank him.

Chapter 30

It was afternoon by the time I stirred under a pile of blankets. Grandpa Bo and Grandma Cora were sitting by my bed. I felt something that I had not known if I would ever feel again. Sweat. I reached up and brushed it from my brow. I felt another source of warmth pressing against me. Tucker was stretched out beside me, his tail thumping against the mattress the moment I woke up.

My grandmother sprung from her chair and scooped me up in her arms. "Oh, George, are you all right?"

I felt fine and knew I was going to recover. I could feel bandages on my right foot, but as warm as the rest of my body felt, my toes still seemed frozen. It would be days before they felt normal—and a miracle that I didn't lose any of them to frostbite. "I'm going to be fine. I've swum in that old pond a hundred times before, just not in the middle of winter. That's all."

"Why is Tucker here?" I said, now holding him close.

My grandma answered. "Thorne asked if you would mind taking care of him again. He said he's got some personal business to attend to, and he thought you might enjoy Tucker's company while you were recovering."

"Where's he going and for how long?"

"He was vague about that. You know by now how private a person he is. But at least a few days, he said."

"Frank Thorne saved my life, you know," I said quietly, stroking Tucker's silky ears.

"Yes, George. We know," Grandpa said, speaking his first words to me. "And Tucker did, too."

Thorne had told them Tucker was the first to hear me hollering for help and was throwing a fit. When he walked outside to find out why the dog was barking and carrying on, Thorne, too, heard my yells and found me at the pond.

Tucker's warm fur was the best medicine I could have hoped for. I held him tight, and I'm not sure which of us was more pleased to be with the other. Tucker let out a mournful little groan that seemed to suggest that some missing part of his soul was put back in place. With each other, we both felt restored, whole.

After a while, I got up and tried to walk. The bottom of my right foot hurt like crazy, so I put on some extra socks to add cushioning. Tucker followed me while I limped around, and I knew that I owed him a great debt for his loyalty. The dog may have very well saved my life. I had no idea how to repay him, or how I would ever thank Frank Thorne.

We ate warm soup at the kitchen table. I was exhausted, but at the same time it felt good just to be alive, safe and warm. More important, it felt good to have Tucker back.

My grandmother insisted that I stay on the sofa for the remainder of the day. I slept away the rest of the evening and most of the following day. Each time I woke from my slumber, Tucker was right there.

By the afternoon of the second day, our county was still shrouded in ice, but at least I was able to convince my grandmother that I was fully recovered.

Chapter 31

Around four o'clock on December 21, I grew restless, wondering if my mother was going to make it. Without phone service, we could only assume that she was headed our way. How she would get through the last thirty miles on these roads was another question.

There was no more putting it off: I needed to start packing. It was hard. I tried to make two piles: things that should go to Minnesota and items that should stay in Kansas. Trouble was, I still couldn't figure out exactly which pile to put myself in. Tucker, standing there in my room wagging his tail, made that choice even harder.

While I was regaining my strength and caring for Tucker, my grandfather had been strangely absent, working on what seemed to be a secret project off-site. When I asked him where he'd gone off to in the maintainer the night before my little mishap at the pond, he'd been vague. Now he was gone again for hours when he wasn't doing the milking or other chores. He wasn't grading roads on this ice, and whatever he was doing seemed to involve daily walks to and from the farm. He did let on that he'd been at

Hank Fisher's house, but what was he up to there? Maybe, I thought, he was working on some secret Christmas present for Grandma Cora and using Hank's tools, though Grandpa did not seem to have enough holiday spirit to be playing elf these days.

My grandmother, though grateful that I was okay, was not too happy about my cattle-rescuing effort, and her mood was as bad as I had ever seen it. Grandpa's project was also irritating her. She said she still had no idea where he'd gone that night, though he'd returned home right after Thorne brought me back to the house.

He had developed a nasty cold that seemed to be turning into a full-blown case of the flu, which he considered nothing more than a nuisance. She was very worried about him and, as I stood there in the kitchen, her voice rose to a point of irritation that was uncommon for her.

"Your grandfather got an extra dose of stubborn and only half a dose of common sense. He'll likely die from pneumonia before spring planting."

"Is he that sick?"

"I've never seen him sicker."

"Well, maybe I should help him?"

"What are you talking about?"

"I feel fine, Grandma. I'm ready to get at it again." For the last few days, I had been exempt from milking duties, but now I was actually

183

eager to help out again. I felt useless sitting around the house, and I certainly did not want to pack.

She turned away in a huff. "Did you think you were a polar bear jumping into that freezing water? You swimming in the pond in the middle of winter and him hiking around on the ice all day—what is wrong with you two?"

"Nothing. I feel fine."

"That's not what I meant, George."

My feet were still tender but much better, and I could walk with almost no pain. I put on my coat and hat, and got Tucker's leash out. He grew excited the minute he saw it, as eager as I was to get outside.

"Where are you two going?" Grandma asked suspiciously, probably worried that I'd disappear with Grandpa.

"Afternoon milking, that's all."

She let out an exasperated sigh. "You are a McCray."

The wind was whistling, but the temperature did not seem unbearable. There was no sign of my grandfather anywhere in the barnyard or the implement shed. The maintainer was gone, but I hadn't heard Grandpa start it up or drive it off the property. Keeping Tucker well heeled on the leash, I pushed open the big sliding door into the milking barn. To my surprise, milking away, like nothing had happened, was Grandpa.

My grandmother was right. He looked tired and whatever he had been working on seemed to have taxed him to exhaustion. I put my hand on his shoulder; otherwise, I'm not sure he would have even noticed us standing there, watching him milk.

He looked up with his blue eyes that were mired in dark black circles. "Well, hello, George. Looks like you are feeling a lot better. I wish I could say the same." He reached over and patted Tucker, too. "Hello, old boy. You're quite the rescue dog, aren't you?"

Skipping all pleasantries, I just asked, "Are you ever going to tell us what you've been working on? I haven't seen much of you for the last couple of days, and Grandma is going crazy wondering."

"I can tell you this much, George. You are going to like it." He coughed several times and offered nothing further by way of an explanation.

Hoping to get a real answer this time, I continued, "Did the maintainer get stuck on the road that night? I didn't see it in the shed."

"Nope. Hank Fisher and I have been working on some alterations. Should be ready—real soon."

"Hank?"

"Hank has an electric generator. With no power, I needed it for the arc welder."

I still didn't understand what he was doing or why he seemed so evasive.

He coughed again and wiped sweat from his brow with the back of his shirtsleeve. "Don't worry, George, you'll see. You know, it was your idea; you said that we had to do something."

It was a two-mile walk to Hank's place and I couldn't imagine walking that distance in this weather, but somehow Grandpa had been making the trip on foot. "Isn't it hard walking that far on the ice?"

He leaned off the milking stool and lifted up one of his legs with a grin. He pulled his pants up above his ankles and showed off the bottoms of his boots. "With these little rascals, it was a nice morning for a walk." He had taken roofing nails and hammered them into the soles.

"It worked?"

"Like a dream. That's where I got the idea, the night before you took your swim."

"What do you mean?" He obviously wanted to surprise me, but I was growing impatient.

He sniffled but did not answer, so I asked, "Do you feel all right?"

"Lousy. I need to get some sleep."

Just then I heard the heavy rumbling of a big engine growing closer; the maintainer had pulled into the driveway. I hurried outside and my grandfather came along behind. Hank Fisher was behind the wheel and he had a giant smile on his face. He got down out of the cab and my grandfather shook his hand.

"Howdy, neighbor."

Hank pointed to the maintainer with pride. "Well, what do you think?"

My grandfather walked around the machine, inspecting. "You did a great job." He stopped at the wheels. It seemed that they had made a few modifications based on my suggestion.

Now I knew what they had been up to. I put my hand on one of the giant rear tires. "Wow!"

Hank stood back, proud of his work. "It was quite a job," he said. "First, I had to find every logging chain I could get my hands on and cut each one to the right length. Welding the logging chains and the clasps together was the easy part. These babies are what took me all night." He ran his hands over hundreds of small steel studs that had been welded onto the chain.

"How did you do it?" I asked.

"I had to cut steel rods into small studs. Then I laid the chain out flat so I could weld the studs onto the chain. I'm hoping the welds will hold. We won't know for sure until we drop the blade."

My grandfather coughed out his thoughts. "We'll need to adjust the grading angle so that we turn the gravel over without pushing it off the road." He pulled a locking pin up, which allowed him to swing the blade so that it was perpendicular to the maintainer. He locked it in place by dropping the pin back down in the hole.

Hank nodded. "We can try to bring the drier

gravel up from the bottom of the roadbed and bury the icier gravel."

"The studs alone won't be enough, but I got another idea that will hopefully make the difference. It's an old trick I learned years ago with deep snow," Grandpa said.

I could feel his excitement growing and I urged him on. "What?"

"When the snow is deep, the maintainer will do just fine on level ground and will do even better on the downhill stretches. It's pushing snow uphill where you need more traction and power than the maintainer can deliver. George, remember that night after you got stuck in the yard? I said I needed to try something. . . ."

"Yes."

"Well, that was it. I tried grading only on the downhill sections and flat sections. In the barnyard, you were trying to push on a slight uphill grade. When I turned down our hill, going west, it was much better. It was almost there. If we only grade going downhill, with the chains and the studs, I think we can make it."

Something was missing. "I don't understand. How can you only grade downhill? What about the uphill sections of the road?"

"Easy. Lift the blade, and drive up the hill without grading, then we'll turn around and go back down the same hill with the blade dropped."

I knew he was right. It would work.

I was pushing my luck, but something inside of me wanted to do this. "Can I take the first go with it?"

My grandfather smiled at my enthusiasm, but he would have none of it.

"George, this is going to be tricky; you need to let me check it out. Maybe you can give it a try later. Driving on ice is different. You should never slam on the brakes; you've got to tap them rapidly. Otherwise, you might skid and rip the studs off the chains."

Realizing that my last foray onto the ice had not turned out well, I only nodded my head and meekly offered, "I can do that."

"I've never done this myself, so I can't really tell you how to do it. My best guess is that we should not grade any deeper than necessary. Hopefully, one to three inches will pull up enough dry material to clear the gravel roads."

"How about the asphalt roads?" Hank asked.

"We'll take it down to the roadbed, if we can."

My old Santa Claus of a grandfather looked like he was about to throw up. He bent over, anticipating nausea, before regaining his composure. "Let's all get a good night's sleep and then start up tomorrow morning. Hank, would you like a ride home? It would give me a chance to test it out."

"You look miserable, Bo. I'll walk back." He lifted his legs to show off the same modification to his shoes. "You've done it a half-dozen times in the last few days—it's my turn."

My grandfather did not argue, and as we headed back into the house, it occurred to me that there was a chance, just a chance, that Cherokee County might still have a Christmas. "Do you think we can grade all the roads in two days?"

My grandfather clapped me on the back. "We've still got problems, George."

I knew what he meant. In those days, there were no salt trucks to help melt the ice or sand trucks to help gain friction. Most vehicles were rear-wheel drive; there were no radial tires and very few people even had snow tires. Without the maintainer pushing the ice off the road, most of our neighbors would be lucky to even get out of their driveways. If they could get out of the driveway, they would not get far.

My grandfather further defined the problem. "There are trees down everywhere, blocking the roads. We'll need chain saws and men to run them and tractors to pull limbs off the road. We would have to have an army of men to get this done before Christmas. We can only do what we can do. We may not get far, but we can get some of the main roads cleared."

If it had been up to me, we would have started a night shift on the spot, with me taking the first turn, but so far my efforts at taking charge had not gone so well.

As I looked at my grandfather that evening, all tired and worn-out, I realized that it just was not going to happen. It wasn't until many years later, when I had my own family, that I realized what he was going through. As children, we feel like the adults in our lives are always pushing us to do more than we want or feel like we should have to do. I didn't understand then that for every inch he pushed me, I had been pushing him the length of an old-fashioned yardstick. He had had enough.

Chapter 32

Twice during the night, I had to get up and tuck my sheets back under the mattress. Laying at the foot of my bed, Tucker had been fidgeting and shifting himself around nervously, and no matter how hard I tried, the blankets did not seem suited for him. With his canine version of tossing and turning going on most of the night, it seemed like the alarm would never go off. Finally, I could stand it no more and rolled out of bed just shy of 4:20 in the morning, armed with a plan. Frankly, Tucker hadn't been the only thing keeping me up. I'd been mulling over an idea and I was ready to put it into action.

The milking I could do on my own—that would give my grandfather a head start. For once, he could sleep in while I got the chores completed and the old diesel engine on the maintainer warmed up for a day of hard work.

After bundling up against the chill in my dark bedroom, I took the leash and a flashlight from the tool drawer in the kitchen, and Tucker and I made our way down to the barn, with only a narrow beam of yellow light to guide us through the ice-covered barnyard.

Without power, we were still milking by hand. My grandfather was right: the Babson Bros. automatic milking machine was an unparalleled invention, and I couldn't wait to get it back. The milk we were pouring out every day was making a frozen mound behind the barn large enough to feed an army of cats. There were raccoon tracks all around the milk mountain, where those resourceful creatures were determined to break off icy chunks for food.

By 7:30 the sun was up, the chores were done, and the ice was cracked, and I started the maintainer to warm it up. I had been expecting my grandfather to join me all morning long but was not too worried when he didn't show. When I got to the house, with a load of firewood in my arms, my grandmother had breakfast waiting for me. "Where's Grandpa?" I asked.

"He spent most of the night in the bathroom. He is exhausted, sick, and won't be out of bed for a week—if he's lucky. Just like I told him."

My heart sank. Of course, I felt sorry for him, but what about the roads? What about Christmas? He had worked so hard and now it was all for nothing? Although I was getting used to the rule book being ignored, surely this was not fair. I'd gotten up extra early just to help Grandpa get out the door and onto the maintainer so that we could get our shifts rolling, but now my plans were wrecked. And so was Christmas for Cherokee County.

Around 8:00, Grandpa stumbled into the kitchen. My disappointment was so deep, I could hardly look up at him.

He interrupted the silence. "Picked an awful time to get sick, didn't I?"

He looked worse and I knew he had no business being out of bed. I mumbled, "People get sick. I did the chores."

"Crack the ice?"

It was embarrassing that he had to ask, but I knew it was a fair question. "Yes, that, too."

"Is that the maintainer I hear running?"

"Yes. I didn't know you were sick."

"Well, you might as well shut it down. Maybe tomorrow."

My grandmother moved into his space like a pouncing cat. "Tomorrow! I don't think so."

Big Bo McCray knew he had met his match, and he quickly turned tail and headed back to the bedroom, mumbling over his shoulder, "We'll see."

I sat at the kitchen table, feeling defeated once more. But while I was running my hand through Tucker's fur, a rough outline of a new and improved plan began forming in my mind.

A week before, I had guided the maintainer up Blackberry Hill to visit Wild Tom Turner. There was a strange feeling in my stomach, an ache just below my solar plexus, as I headed up that driveway that led to Turner's trailer. Many years later, I would come to recognize that dull aching feeling in my stomach as the way my conscience tries to tell me to think again. Now, for the second time in a week, I experienced that feeling, knowing that I was about to do something I should not do, but willing to do it anyway. If they got really mad at me, what would they do— banish me to Minnesota?

After I shoved my arms through the sleeves of my coat and pulled on my hat and gloves, Tucker and I headed back outside. Once inside the implement barn, I sat on the seat of that main-tainer, and instead of shutting it down, I did what I had no business doing. After all, I am a McCray.

"Tucker, get up here with me!" I moved over and he situated himself in the bed I had made for him.

With the maintainer in reverse, I backed out of the barn. Tucker and I were headed out to clear the roads of Cherokee County. We didn't bother looking back.

Chapter 33

With my feet parked by the steel heater that blasted warm air from the bottom of the maintainer, and my coat buttoned to the top, I shifted the transmission into first gear and eased out of the barnyard. As a renegade road maintainer, there was no stopping at the house for food or drink. I was sure Grandma Cora could hear the big machine go by, and that she'd see me from the kitchen and tell my grandfather, but no one was about to chase me down on this ice.

At the end of the driveway, I turned east and headed down the hill. The maintainer was sure-footed with the chains and homemade studs that Hank Fisher had spent the night welding, but the real test was dropping the blade.

I wanted to wait for a flat spot, with shallow ditches on each side, to test out the modifications, but I would be on a downhill slope for a while. Taking a deep breath, I grabbed the adjusting lever and let the blade down easy, an inch at a time.

The maintainer jerked to the right, causing me to lose control just as I had in the driveway a few days before. I panicked for fear that I would flip the maintainer, and I did the worst thing possible and applied the brakes too hard. The maintainer started to skid out of control. Determined not to fail before I even got to the bottom of McCray's Hill, I remembered what Grandpa had told me. While it seemed counter-intuitive, I tried releasing and tapping the brakes. The maintainer started to straighten and the skidding stopped. Pushing the blade farther down to the road surface gave me even more stability. I could hear the sweet sound of ice coming up and off the road. I turned around and looked behind me.

The maintainer was the world's largest ice cube maker, spewing chunks of ice off each end of the blade! Grandpa was right—the momentum of going down the hill was just what we needed.

I was ready to spring my plan into action.

First stop was our nearest neighbor to the east, Frank Thorne. After I bladed the ice right off his driveway, I jumped down and ran to his door.

I was out of breath, but when Thorne came to the door, I blurted out, "I wanted to thank you."

"It was nothing, kid." He seemed to be avoiding my gaze. "How are you doing? You were in pretty bad shape last time I saw you."

"I'm all better now. It was nice to have this guy around to keep me company," I said, nodding at Tucker.

"I had some things I needed to do and I couldn't let him tag along—thanks for watching him again."

He reached down and patted Tucker on the head.

"It was no problem."

"Hang on to him a little longer. I can see he's enjoying riding around with you on that big machine. What do you want, George?"

Excited, I struggled to get my words out. "I was wondering . . . could I get . . . your help on something?"

He looked at me suspiciously. "A McCray asking a Thorne for help?"

There was a lot of hurt in his words, but I pointed out to him an undeniable truth. "Mr. Thorne, you already helped a McCray the other day. You saved my life."

From the gleam in his eyes, I could tell that he was a little proud of himself—deservedly. "What do you have on your mind?"

Once I had explained the problem, he looked at me in a curious way and said, "Stay here." He shut the door and I waited in the cold morning air for him to return. When he did, he was dressed warmly, a chain saw in one hand and the keys to his old brown truck in the other.

Chapter 34

When my grandfather awoke from a nap later that afternoon, my grandmother insisted that he get up and out of bed and eat in the kitchen. He told me later how her mood had changed. One minute she'd exiled him to the bedroom, and now she wanted him up and about. Perhaps to make sure he stayed in bed, she had not shared with him that I had headed out of the driveway on the maintainer earlier that morning.

Her hands on her hips, she hovered over the bed and said, "Bo, you're a no-good lazy man. Get up out of that bed this minute and come into the kitchen for some food. Besides, there's something I want you to see."

The look on his face when he came to the kitchen window and peered out into the barnyard must have been pure astonishment. He was looking out at the "army" he and Hank said we would need to clear the roads of Cherokee County: thirteen crews of men in trucks with chain saws and fourteen tractors with driveway blades or tow chains to haul off logs. Earlier that morning, Frank Thorne had helped me and Tucker spread the word from farm to farm, and now everyone was saying the same thing: *Let's get the roads cleared for Christmas.* The McCray farm was headquarters for this effort. It was like a contest to see who could help the most. Each driveway that Thorne and I had cleared that morning netted us another volunteer road maintainer. Although it was still well below freezing, working conditions were decent. No more snow or ice was coming down, so it wasn't getting any worse.

The word eventually spread all the way to town and the phone and power company crews got into the spirit, too.

My plan was to make the first priority clearing the roads of downed trees and branches so the utility trucks could make their repairs and the maintainer could pass through. Once the maintainer cut its initial eight-foot swath straight down the middle of the road, the much smaller farm tractors could find enough traction to take another foot or two with their driveway blades. In this fashion, the maintainer, in tandem with four or five tractors, could clear the roads in one pass. Without the maintainer leading the way, none of this would have worked.

Tucker and I kept the maintainer going all day on December 22 and December 23. Thorne changed his mind and decided to take some night shifts on the maintainer.

The road crews worked through the nights, as

well. Along the sides of the roads of Cherokee County were stacks of wood and a foot-high pile of ice. On the third day, Christmas Eve, we were blessed with warmer weather that aided our efforts, and more houses, including our own, had their phone and power service restored. Things were just about getting back to normal.

Frank Thorne seemed to naturally take over the job as manager of the auxiliary road crew. I was glad to hand over the reins. It appeared he had a better ability to manage others than he did to manage his own life. My grandfather said that during the war, by all accounts Thorne had been a good soldier. Perhaps he got a little of his pride and confidence back by stepping up and taking responsibility for the crew.

Grandma Cora and other local women kept our kitchen busy with pots of coffee and massive amounts of food for the hungry workers. As I worked the maintainer, Tucker remained with me up in the cab, and I couldn't imagine working a shift without him. It was fantastic having him back with me again—even if he wasn't really my dog.

In the early afternoon of December 24, I returned home from my last shift and more fell than got off the maintainer. Everyone had gone home. The parking areas where our road crew had assembled were empty. Instead of climbing back onto the maintainer to take over, my grandfather just put his arms around my shoulders and said, "We're done. It's good enough."

I started to protest that there were still roads to be cleared, so he repeated himself. "It's good enough. I think you can take a lot of the credit for giving Christmas back to Cherokee County, son. Come inside. There's someone who would like to see you."

There were no cars other than ours parked in the driveway, so I was surprised that I had a visitor. Tucker and I made our way up to the house. After kicking off my muddy boots, I opened the back door and walked into the kitchen, with my grandfather following right behind.

Standing by the sink were my mother and my two sisters. They had decided to take the bus from Minneapolis to Crossing Trails. Thanks to all of our work the last two days, Hank and his wife were able to bring them the rest of the way in their car. My grandparents knew they were on their way, but they wanted it to be a surprise. It was the best Christmas present I could get.

Tears streamed down my mom's face. Not waiting for me to come to her, she quickly closed the space between us and held me in her arms, shifting her weight back and forth in a rocking motion. She held me so tightly I wasn't sure I could breathe. She just kept saying over and over, "Oh, honey, oh, honey . . ."

Her wet tears felt warm on my cold face. "George, you're freezing." She cupped my chin in her soft hands as if to warm me up, the way she'd done since I was a small child. "I just can't believe what you've done! I'm proud of you. Your sisters and I missed you so much."

Her warmth flowed through my veins and invigorated my spirit, but the strong emotions I felt left me tongue-tied. "Thanks, Mom" was all I could manage. I reached down and hugged Tucker. "This is our dog!" It may not have been the truth, but that was how I felt. Tucker had become a McCray.

Before I knew it, my two sisters, Trisha and Hannah, had their arms around me, too; I realized just how much I had missed the rest of my family. They kept looking at me and saying, "George, you look different."

My grandmother stood back and gave us the space we needed to reconnect. "Sit down and rest! Eat." She herded everyone to the dining-room table, which was covered with food.

For the first time since June 14, 1962, my whole family was sitting down together, laughing and feeling joy. The absence of my father still hung in the air, but it was not weighing us down.

We sat at the table for a good long while, chatting and eating way more than we needed, as if we were making up for months of missed family dinners. Periodically, my grandmother would go into the kitchen, where she would make and receive telephone calls to and from friends and neighbors. We couldn't hear much of her conversation from the dining room, but apparently there was a lot of catching up to do. She spent most of the afternoon chatting on the phone with our neighbors—though she acted so secretive that I started to think it was her turn to be up to something.

We enjoyed recounting the day-to-day, seemingly insignificant details that had made up our lives over the last few months—the unreliable gas stove in the new house; the day a kid at school flooded the boys' bathroom; the traffic outside of Minneapolis; how I milked the cows without the help of the Babson Brothers, and much more. Of course, Mom wanted to hear every last detail of my fall into the frozen pond, and all about Tucker's heroics. I made sure to also give Frank Thorne credit. As we talked, Tucker made his way around the room and took his time getting to know my mother and my sisters, with the help of the table scraps they slipped to him.

As the afternoon came to an end and we finally began clearing the table and cleaning up the dishes, something wholly unexpected occurred. It started with a knock on the back door. It being a country home, no one ever came to the front door.

When I opened the door, there stood Hank

Fisher and his wife. "Well, if it isn't the youngest maintainer!" Hank boomed, shaking my hand.

Before I even had a chance to ask him in, our neighbors to the west, William Foster and his family, appeared at the door. Both the Fishers and the Fosters said they wanted to thank the McCrays for keeping their roads cleared. As they stepped into the kitchen, there were more knocks on the door and more cars arriving. One after another, nearly all our neighbors and many members of the volunteer road crew showed up.

After six or seven cars arrived and no one left, it became clear to me that these were not random instances of neighborly gratitude, with the Fishers and Fosters and others just happening to show up at the same time. Grandma Cora's phone calls! She was behind all this.

Tucker wound his way through our now-crowded house, with overflow in the kitchen, the dining room, and the living room, where the Christmas tree that had seemed so bare only a few days before was suddenly now wrapped in bright lights, surrounded by packages decked out in Christmas colors of green and red. Mrs. Slater, most of the Rather family (Sherry was home with a healthy baby boy), and even a quiet but smiling Frank Thorne became part of the crowd. Most of the gifts that had materialized beneath the tree were presents from grateful residents of Cherokee County.

Many of our neighbors recognized Tucker from the hours he spent beside me on the maintainer. Hank Fisher gave him an affectionate pat and then looked up at me.

"George, if firemen need Dalmatians, I guess maintainers need Irish Setters!" Frank Thorne, who'd been standing within earshot of Hank, caught my eye at that moment and nodded. I nodded back, though I felt a wave of sadness as I knew my time with Tucker was running out—as was my time with all the good people who surrounded me now.

If Grandpa Bo was still feeling a little tired after his go-round with the flu and his night shifts on the maintainer, his energy was now revitalized by the crowd of well-wishers. While he may not have uttered twenty words to many of his neighbors before, tonight Grandpa spoke freely of how I had single-handedly saved his herd of cattle from certain death and how proud he was of me for organizing the emergency road-clearing efforts. He told everyone he could get to listen that it was my persistence that had cleared the roads of ice.

My family allowed my grandfather his proud boasts, though I was a bit embarrassed at all the attention, as any thirteen-year-old boy would have been. Still, I like to think that my mother and I both realized that night that she had not left me "behind" in Kansas. Over the last four months, and particularly in the last few days, I had moved "ahead"—far, far ahead.

Once the last guest had parted with his or her wish for a Merry Christmas, the evening milking was finished, and every dish was cleaned and put away, Grandma put on her coat and told us to bundle up. "We're going into town." It seemed there was one more surprise she'd cooked up.

I couldn't bear to leave my friend behind. "Can I bring Tucker?"

"Sure, but he'll have to wait in the car for part of the time."

When we did not move fast enough, she ordered, "Load up, now!"

Driving into town in Grandma's Impala, all crunched together, family and dog, we had no idea what she was up to. Apparently, my grandfather did not know, either. She issued directions as we went. "Left at the light. Now keep going. Go straight to the school."

The Crossing Trails Central School parking lot was full. When we got out of the car, my grandmother clutched a grocery sack so close to her that one wondered if the contents came from a bank vault. Before she got out of the car, my mother cracked open her window. We left Tucker resting on the backseat, burrowed beneath a warm wool blanket. He was glad to be included in our trip to town and seemed to understand that not all errands were dog errands.

Within moments, it was clear what Grandma Cora had been up to that night. With a little organizing from the women in our community, the town of Crossing Trails patched together a spontaneous pageant to celebrate the holiday that almost was not. We collected at the Crossing Trails Central School auditorium.

As the audience found their seats, some grade-schoolers on stage stumbled, rather than led us, through Christmas carols. Still, like most of the adults in the crowd, my mom and grandparents broke into wide grins at the sound of children singing. When we got ready to sit down, my grandmother, still holding firm to that grocery sack, grabbed my hand.

"Not you, George. You are coming with me."

It was clear that she was on some kind of mission as she led me to the door of the boys' bathroom and thrust the sack at me. "Put this on and go find your teacher—she's waiting for you backstage. And hurry. We don't have much time," she said before she disappeared back down the hallway. I peeked in the sack and discovered that Grandma Cora had hurriedly sewn together a Santa Claus costume. I pulled it on, including a hat with a white beard attached, and then turned to the mirror. I looked absolutely ridiculous.

"Hey, George—can you give me a hand?" I thought I was alone in the bathroom until I heard the voice of my classmate Eddie Sampson, who was trying to struggle into an elf suit. Suddenly, I felt less ridiculous.

It turned out that the centerpiece of that night's show was the production of a Christmas play by the sixth- and seventh-graders. Performing the lines that I had never bothered to memorize, while wearing my Santa ensemble, would take far more courage than driving a maintainer in a blizzard or rescuing a few cows from a frozen pond. Then Mrs. Weeks put me at ease as she handed me the script.

"We're only doing the last act, and you can read your lines." She walked out onto the stage and the cast of *Santa and the Lost Elves* followed behind. Well, I thought as I shuffled out onto the stage with my heart pounding, if a tough guy like Eddie could wear red tights in public, then I could wear Grandma's Saint Nick costume and read, a skill I had down pat.

Mrs. Weeks stepped up to the microphone, summarized the first two acts for the audience, and then concluded, "With the school closing, our actors have not had time to memorize their lines, so their dramatic interpretation of Act Three will be read. Santa Claus is played by George McCray."

My sister Trisha embarrassed me terribly by whooping and hollering at the mention of my name. That actually was the worst part. In fact, with the summary of the first two acts inserted, and with all of us practically speed-reading our lines as kids tend to do, the play was bearable and mercifully short.

As I offered my final "Ho, ho, ho and have a Merry Christmas," we exited the stage to enthusiastic applause. My friend Mary Ann was dressed as an angel; her hair was pulled back behind her plastic halo, and when I looked at her, I thought she played the part well.

She grabbed my arm playfully. "Good job, George! You didn't fall asleep once."

"That's only because you didn't have any lines," I shot back.

With no warning, she leaned toward me and kissed me on the cheek and whispered, "I am going to miss you."

Thankfully, she darted off and did not see me playing the part of George, the red-faced Santa Claus.

After I changed out of my costume and said some hurried but wistful goodbyes to a few friends—all of whom swore they'd be my Kansas pen pals forever—I found my family by the main door and we made our way out to Grandma's car. I ran ahead to let Tucker out and then we circled back to the join the group. Suddenly, there was a shout from across the parking lot. I assumed it was just another neighborly well-wisher.

"Hey, George!"

It was Frank Thorne. He walked toward us, holding a package.

My grandmother gave Thorne a big hug, which surprised me, until I remembered the role she'd played in helping Thorne shake off his old ways and take some steps forward—some very large steps, indeed.

"Our George was in the Christmas play. He was the star."

Thorne looked at me approvingly. "I saw. A damn, I mean darn, good Santa Claus."

He reached out and shook my hand. "I want to thank you, George. What you and your family have done for me means more than you can imagine. I want you to have this." He handed me the package he had been carrying.

I took the package but did not know what to say or do.

"Go ahead, open it."

The paper came off easily enough, but in the dim light of the parking lot, it took me a moment to understand what it was that I held. It was the picture of Thorne and my father that had hung on his wall. I swallowed hard and held out my hand to shake his. "Thank you, Mr. Thorne. I'm pleased to have a picture of you and my dad."

His words were soft and gentle this time, without the old edge I'd first encountered. "You can call me Frank. Your dad was a fine man. Best friend I ever had."

211

Thorne had taken many a wrong turn and made more than one bad decision, but in a few short weeks I learned how good a man he truly was. I had Thorne wrong, all wrong. He taught me an important life lesson that December—that rushing to judgment rarely worked in anyone's favor.

While I was grateful for the picture and the kind words, what he said next meant more.

Thorne stared down at his boots for a few seconds and then looked up at me. There was a glint in the eyes that I could only describe as profound determination. Tucker pulled on his leash and whined. I let go and he made his way over to Thorne, who bent down to pet the dog, then buried his face in his fur. When he stood up, there were small tears in his eyes.

"George, I've got a job. First job I've had in years. It's at the plant, putting together Fords in Kansas City. That's why I asked you to hang on to the dog a few extra days, because I had to make some arrangements. Red here needs to be on the farm. I wonder if you and your grandparents would mind taking him for me?" Before I could answer, he continued, "For good, this time."

I was leaving for Minnesota in a few days, but I was counting on my mom letting me take the dog with me, if not on this trip then at least on the next one. I looked to my grandfather with every ounce of *want* I could muster, but it didn't take much convincing.

Before I could say a word, my grandfather nodded his head approvingly. "Frank, we'll do it. We could use a good dog."

Thorne nodded too, as if to reassure me. "Go ahead, George. You'd be doing me a favor."

I knelt down to scratch Tucker. He cocked his head at Thorne, then looked back at me. It seemed that Tucker understood. He looked at Thorne one more time and barked.

"Stay," Frank said to him, with a little smile. "It's all going to be okay—Tucker."

As I felt Tucker's cold wet nose and warm fur on my face, I did not understand what rule allowed us to have this dog, but I felt a gratitude that seeped into the very marrow of my bones. As excited as I was to get Tucker one step closer to being mine, it was going to be very disappointing if I couldn't take him with me.

"Mr. Thorne—Frank . . . ," I stammered, looking up to thank him, but he was already walking away, heading back to his truck. The old engine turned over and with a final wave he drove off, leaving me stunned. I held Tucker like I would never let him go. As I got to my feet, I tried to think of a thousand ways to thank Frank Thorne, but I didn't get the chance. The next morning, his worldly possessions were loaded into his truck. He got in it and drove off without saying goodbye, never to be seen again.

Chapter 35

When we got home, Mom kept hugging me and asking for more details about everything I had been doing the last few weeks. Sitting on the living room floor, I answered her questions as best I could.

"Weren't you scared of driving that big old maintainer?"

"At the beginning. But I got used to it after the first few days."

"Tell me again about the ice."

Tucker chose that moment to offer a friendly bark at Mom. She ran her hands through his fur. "I know just how you felt, Tucker. Some days I was so worried about George, too."

My sisters and grandparents joined us in the living room to open a few presents, as we'd always done on Christmas Eve. It was quite late, but this was a McCray family tradition. I didn't feel the urge to unwrap anything, though, since to me Tucker was the best package under the tree.

It was hard to believe that he was mine. Every few minutes I hugged my beautiful red dog and let him know how pleased I was to have him back on the farm for good.

My mother sat in the chair closest to the fireplace and stared at all of the packages. Even though there was a smile on her face, her eyes still looked sad. I think we all had the same hollow feeling in our stomachs. With all the commotion surrounding our impromptu open house, followed by the excitement of the Christmas pageant and then Thorne's "gift" to me, I'd managed to avoid confronting the reality we all now faced together: the first Christmas we would share without my father.

She caught me looking at her and said, "You have a lot of thank-you notes to write, young man."

Around midnight, with yawns and droopy eyes, we opened the packages from our neighbors and friends, saving the more personal family gifts for Christmas Day. My sisters played the roles of Santa's helpers and read each gift tag aloud, all of us chuckling at how many packages were for Tucker. "Here's another one —For the Big Red Dog!" There were many presents for me, as well.

Of course, I can't remember all of the gifts that showed up that night, but there were a few that stood out, including a thank-you note from Mrs. Slater with a picture of Tucker she had drawn and a little red plastic dog Christmas ornament that I still hang on the tree.

With the fire burning warm and the gift opening behind us, I felt very content with Tucker and the rest of my family all in one room. As I became even more relaxed, I remembered how comforting it was to just experience family conversation, without listening to individual words. What they said didn't matter. It was like a symphony—the sounds of the particular instruments were lost to the larger pattern and movements of sound. Although it had been a very long time since I had heard it, and one important instrument was missing, it was still an old familiar concerto that played through our home once again that night.

I drifted off listening to my sisters and my mother sitting around the table struggling to find the shapes that would fit into a still unknown pattern. The last words I remembered were "Grandma hasn't touched last year's puzzle."

Chapter 36

On Christmas day, while Grandma and my mother made breakfast, Trisha and Hannah gave the McCray men their first present for Christmas day—helping with the chores. Even with electricity, it still took us over two hours to do the milking. Watching Trisha and Hannah try to strap the Babson Bros. automatic milking machine onto a cow not only made me feel like an old pro but kept me laughing for most of the morning. Grandpa and I could knock our routine out in an hour and a half, but I doubted with as much cheer.

Breakfast was served in the dining room. Special occasions, like Christmas morning, usually brought forth the same menu of warm buttermilk biscuits, smoked bacon, and scrambled eggs piled high on an antique dish. Our appetites were intact and before long we pushed away from the table content.

We were all trying very hard to be thankful for what we had and not dwell on what we had lost. But try as we did, the excitement from yesterday wore off and we were all faced with the difficult realization that John McCray, our father, son, or spouse, was gone. It was one of many firsts that we had to get through.

With a wet dish towel in my hand and the breakfast dishes almost behind me, my mom took me aside. She handed me a sack and whispered into my ear, "Merry Christmas." I opened the bag to find that it was full of my favorite oatmeal cookies.

"Thanks, Mom."

She gave me a big hug and said, "George, you've turned into such a nice young man, but I still think I am going to miss my boy."

Of course, I beamed when she called me a man.

"Your dad and I are both so proud of you." She held me tightly a minute longer before she took my hand and said, "I've missed you. It's going to be good having you home with me again."

I didn't know what to say. There was no use telling her that I was torn in two about leaving. It would have broken her heart. Still, she could tell that something was bothering me.

"Come on, George, we've got family presents to open. It's Christmas!" She wiped her eyes quickly and headed for the living room.

We were about to gather around the tree, but we could not find my grandfather. Grandma Cora yelled for him several times, but he did not appear. She went to the bedroom to look for him. When she returned, her energy seemed drained and she asked us to be patient; Grandpa Bo would need just a few more minutes. When he finally came into the living room, he looked so worn-out that I thought he must have journeyed a hundred miles from that back bedroom. In some ways, I suppose he had.

Before he sat down, he placed under the tree a package wrapped in brown paper, cut from a grocery sack.

Typically, we unwrapped presents in a frenzy, but this year we took our time, offering polite thank-yous along the way. Hannah handed the gifts out one at a time. Eventually, the presents dwindled down to that little brown package.

Hannah cried out, "We forgot this one!" She held the last little brown paper package in her hand. "It says, 'To Tucker, from the McCray family.'"

She passed it over to me. "Here, George, you open it for Tucker."

We were all excited to have something to offer our newest family member. His brushed red coat was perfect for Christmas and his fine figure adorned the living room floor with as much flare as any ornament on the tree. I pulled the simple wrapping off the package. I gasped.

My grandfather had carefully sculpted the most beautiful dog collar I had ever seen. It was made of soft brown leather and he had burned in the words TUCKER MCCRAY. There were brass rivets to hold the buckle in place. I put the collar around Tucker and it stayed there for many years to come.

As everyone dispersed about the house, Grandma called me into the kitchen. She and Grandpa were standing by the sink. Grandma spoke first.

"Your grandfather has another gift for you. It's a going-away present."

"George, I want you to know how much I appreciate all of the help you've given us these last few weeks. You're going to be a tough hand to replace." He then handed me a box wrapped in red paper. There was a handwritten note that went with it, scrawled with words in my grandfather's old-fashioned handwriting:

To: *The best maintainer this family ever had!*
From: *Grandma and Grandpa McCray*

I unwrapped the box and lifted the lid. It was my grandfather's tin cup that had sat by that kitchen sink for so many years. It would have gone to my father, but instead it came to me.

I stared at the gift for a long time, strangely touched by the simple tin cup that had been handed down from father to son for four generations. My grandfather must have been holding two very different thoughts in his head at the same time. He was glad to pass this piece of family history to me, but how sad he must have felt to skip a generation.

Trying to break the solemn mood, I put the ancient tin cup to my lips, drank the imaginary contents dry, and let out a long "Ahh."

The moment touched Grandpa. The cup was not valuable to anyone else, but it signified something important to him. I drew nearer to give him a hug. "Thank you, Grandpa." He held me tight in his still strong arms. Of course, I was thanking him for much more than a cup.

Many years later, my mother told me something that had never crossed my mind. Losing my father had broken Bo's heart, but on that Christmas day, the thought of me packing up and leaving just about finished him off.

My grandmother spoke up. "Now that you're an official road maintainer, you'll need a good cup to drink from. That cup has sat by our sink for sixty years; now it can sit by your sink in Minnesota."

Chapter 37

Even on Christmas day, there were chores to do. We trusted Tucker around the cows now, but I still kept him tethered with his new collar and long leash in the barn while I milked. I insisted on taking both shifts that day, but I had a new partner that afternoon.

"You didn't think I knew how to do this, did you?" My mom swung the Babson Bros. milker into place.

"You're good, Mom, but I think you need a little more practice."

She looked up from the milker. "I've got two more days to learn, before we leave."

I tried to smile. "That's right."

She seemed to be testing the waters with her next comment. "I am looking forward to being your mother again."

"You don't need to worry, Mom. Grandma has been taking good care of me." It didn't occur to me how it might hurt her to hear this.

"I'm glad for that . . ." Her words trailed off and she worked quietly until we were finished and walked back to the house.

The day's activities and a dinner of turkey and

dressing made us all tired. That evening, I just read and once more enjoyed the presence of my family and my dog. My sisters gestured to the puzzle table. "Grandma, why don't you help us?"

Grandma Cora stood in the dining room with a pained look on her face. I don't think she knew how to go back to that table, where she had passed so many hours with my father, without feeling his absence. It was safer to avoid it. When she didn't answer, it was clear to me that the idea of puzzling was causing her discomfort.

"I don't think she wants to do the puzzle," I blurted out.

Apparently my observation did not help matters. She turned and walked away. My sisters realized what they had done and raced after her into the kitchen, with my mother close behind.

There were tearful sobs and apologies. It was quiet for a very long time, and I began to wonder what they were doing and why it was taking so long. My grandfather set down his newspaper and was shifting his weight nervously.

Suddenly, my grandmother's clear-as-a-bell voice echoed through the house. "Come on, girls."

Seconds later the McCray women emerged from the kitchen, composed and determined. They stopped for a moment, and with a measure of strength and beauty that I would never forget, my grandmother spoke just two simple words. "It's time."

They sat down at the puzzle table, grasped hands, and closed their eyes. They were silent for a few moments and I felt a knot form in my throat. When my grandmother opened her eyes, they were clear and alive. An unclaimed joyful presence seemed to flow in the room like a refreshing spring breeze.

She tucked a stray white hair behind one ear, smiled, and said, "We have work to do."

With eight hands they made fast progress.

Around 11:00 that night, with the last embers of the fire pulsing with a warm dry heat, Hannah calmly observed, "Finished."

I was half asleep on the sofa, but I smiled from my daze.

Grandma Cora motioned to me. "Come see, George."

Rolling off the sofa, I went over to the puzzle table. What I saw took me by surprise. It was an aerial photograph of our farm cut into a puzzle.

Grandma grabbed my hand and said, "You know, George, your father liked to give me puzzles that were darn near impossible to put together. This time he almost did it."

It was late, so I just leaned over and kissed each of the four women I loved most in the world on the cheek and went to bed. Within a few minutes, my sisters and Tucker followed behind. It seemed that he, too, needed a good night's rest. Tomorrow I would have to finish packing. Again, it seemed that some rule was strangely off-kilter. Young men should not have to leave the homes they love—nor should they be separated from their parents.

I couldn't sleep. Around midnight, I heard voices coming up through the floor grate. Like me, they were all wondering what would come next.

My mother's voice was agitated. "He is just playing at packing. He hasn't asked about his new room, our house, or his new school. Don't you think if he wanted to go, he would say something?"

My grandmother tried to reassure her. "Sarah, this is the only home he has ever known. He can be both sad to leave and happy to be back with you at the same time."

My mother seemed to know exactly how I felt. "I don't think that's it; it's clear to me that he doesn't want to go."

"Of course he wants to be with you and his sisters."

"Has he ever said anything about not wanting to go?"

My grandmother was silent for a few moments before she did something I never thought possible. She lied. "No, honey, George would never say that."

Finally, my grandfather asked in his to-the-point way, "Is he old enough to decide on his own?"

My mother's voice cracked. "I won't do that to him. It puts him in an awful place: choosing between people he loves. This isn't about me and my needs. It's about what's best for him."

I heard the old kitchen chairs being pushed away from the table. Tired, weary, and familiar-sounding steps creaked on the staircase. I closed my eyes, the way kids do when they pretend to be sleeping and a parent comes into the room, just as my mother pushed open the door.

I felt her weight on the bed as she came and sat beside me. She ran her hands through my hair for a few moments. Tucker got up from his resting spot on my bed and walked over me to get to her for a pat, which gave me the perfect excuse to "wake up."

I sat up and my mom took me in her arms like she was just giving me a big goodnight hug. She held on to me for a very long time. It was a hug she knew would have to last for many years to come.

"George, I want to talk to you. Are you awake enough to listen?"

Chapter 38

My mother's winter visits back to the farm in the years to come were some of the best times of my young life. Even after my sisters were married and had families of their own, Mom faithfully returned every December for the holidays. I spent Thanksgiving and six weeks of the summer in Minnesota. In between, we exchanged endless letters, spoke regularly by phone, and made extra trips when we could. There may have been some distance between us, but there was no lack of connection.

It's been a long time now since she made her last Christmas visit to our farm in Kansas. A very long time. That's what makes today so special.

She should be arriving any minute now. I have Tucker's collar, my grandfather's tin cup, and the last puzzle my father gave Grandma Cora, all sitting here beside me. Mom's memory is fading. The doctor encouraged us to show her objects when we recount the past to her. It was up to me to be the curator for this exhibit, to put together just the right pieces from our family museum.

When the time is right, I want her to sit by the fire, hear our stories, and be comforted by our history—to know how important her place is. There are things I want to tell her, things I want her to understand. I don't know what she remembers, what is lost, and how much more time I have to let her know how I feel. I practice the story one last time. . . .

Grandpa was the road maintainer for Cherokee County. His name was Bo McCray and my grandmother's name was Cora. After Dad died, I stayed here on the farm, with my dog, Tucker, to live with my grandparents. They helped bring me up. Of all the courageous people from that period in my life, my mom was one of the bravest. She let me stay here because she knew it would have hurt me too much to leave.

Having children of my own, I know how hard it must have been for her. Sometimes the strongest people in the world are the ones who let go so the rest of us can hang on.

In the winter of 1962, I learned how to be a maintainer. Some might think that it wasn't an important job, but I'm convinced that most of the important tasks in our lives all amount to the same thing: clearing away the burdens that block our way.

Tucker and I had five more warm summers and cold winters together before he became an old man of a dog. Many of those winters had snow days, but nothing like the snow we experienced that year. How it piled up.

Within a few years, I was driving Grandpa's old Ford truck to school and dating a young woman. Mary Ann had been my best friend on the bus for years. She was an angel in that Christmas pageant. When the pageant was over, I looked at her in a different way. I am still looking at her like that forty years later.

Grandma Cora told me that Tucker could hear me approaching in that Ford truck from miles away. He would begin pacing the back of the porch, his tail wagging furiously and letting out little happy greeting barks when I pulled into the driveway. He was a beautiful dog—the dog of a lifetime.

When I graduated from high school, I went to Vietnam. Tucker and Cherokee County were left behind on a Friday and I would not return for two very long years.

Tucker hardly left the back porch for months. He assumed I would return home after school, just like I did most every other day of his life with us. He thought there was a rule. I knew how he felt—day after day, hoping that someone you love is going to come, as always, right through that back kitchen door.

On an April morning, Tucker became restless. Grandma Cora watched as he got up and looked south to Kill Creek. He whined and ran off for

Mack's Ground. Maybe he was looking for me. Maybe he just knew his end was near and wanted to spend his last days in full flower.

People saw him all over the county that week and they would say, "Isn't that George McCray's big red dog?" They would call and let Grandma know that he had been roaming far afield, but no one could ever catch up to him.

After a week, he returned home exhausted but content. He collapsed on the back porch and never got up again. He died there, having led a full and happy life. A truer and better friend I have never known. He was a gift. I will always miss old Tucker.

Grandma Cora and Grandpa Bo found it hard to say goodbye to him, too. They carried him to Mack's Ground and buried him by the lake, the place where he was the happiest. He still rests there. Grandpa made a simple wooden bench and placed it beside the lake. To this day, my family and I can walk to Mack's Ground, sit by the lake, skip stones, and, when the weather permits, dangle our feet in the cool water. Sometimes I tell them about Tucker. His collar has hung in the barn all these years.

I've got it here beside me now.

Grandpa and Grandma are long gone, too. I miss them more than words can tell. When I come in from a day of running McCray's Dairy, from working in the barns and meadows and fields that still surround our farm, I take a long drink from this old tin cup that I still keep by the sink. When it's empty and I've quenched my thirst, I say "Ahh," long and slow.

There is one last thing I will share with my mother. I will tell her that I've had a good life on the farm pictured in Grandma Cora's puzzle by trusting in my father's simple rule: no matter how much falls on us, we keep plowing ahead.

That's the only way to keep the roads clear.

Center Point Publishing
600 Brooks Road ● PO Box 1
Thorndike ME 04986-0001 USA

(207) 568-3717

US & Canada:
1 800 929-9108
www.centerpointlargeprint.com